Harriet E. Wilson

OUR NIG

Sketches from the Life of a Free Black

DOVER PUBLICATIONS, INC.
Mineola, New York

Bibliographical Note

This Dover edition, first published in 2005, is an unabridged republication of the work originally published in 1859 by George C. Rand and Avery, Boston.

Library of Congress Cataloging-in-Publication Data

Wilson, Harriet E., 1808–ca. 1870.
 Our Nig : sketches from the life of a free Black / Harriet E. Wilson.
  p. cm.
 ISBN-13: 978-0-486-44561-8 (pbk.)
 ISBN-10: 0-486-44561-5 (pbk.)
 1. African American women domestics—Fiction. 2. African American women—Fiction. 3. Free African Americans—Fiction. 4. New England—Fiction. 5. Racism—Fiction. I. Title: Sketches from the life of a free Black. II. Title.
PS3334.W3909 2005
813'.3—dc22

              2005045982

Manufactured in the United States by LSC Communications
44561509 2018
www.doverpublications.com

OUR NIG;

OR,

Sketches from the Life of a Free Black,

IN A TWO-STORY WHITE HOUSE, NORTH.

SHOWING THAT SLAVERY'S SHADOWS FALL EVEN THERE.

BY "OUR NIG."

" I know
That care has iron crowns for many brows;
That Calvaries are everywhere, whereon
Virtue is crucified, and nails and spears
Draw guiltless blood; that sorrow sits and drinks
At sweetest hearts, till all their life is dry;
That gentle spirits on the rack of pain
Grow faint or fierce, and pray and curse by turns;
That hell's temptations, clad in heavenly guise
And armed with might, lie evermore in wait
Along life's path, giving assault to all." — HOLLAND.

BOSTON:
PRINTED BY GEO. C. RAND & AVERY.
1859.

PREFACE.

In offering to the public the following pages, the writer confesses her inability to minister to the refined and cultivated, the pleasure supplied by abler pens. It is not for such these crude narrations appear. Deserted by kindred, disabled by failing health, I am forced to some experiment which shall aid me in maintaining myself and child without extinguishing this feeble life. I would not from these motives even palliate slavery at the South, by disclosures of its appurtenances North. My mistress was wholly imbued with *southern* principles. I do not pretend to divulge every transaction in my own life, which the unprejudiced would declare unfavorable in comparison with treatment of legal bondmen; I have purposely omitted what would most provoke shame in our good anti-slavery friends at home.

My humble position and frank confession of errors will, I hope, shield me from severe criticism. Indeed, defects are so apparent it requires no skilful hand to expose them.

I sincerely appeal to my colored brethren universally for patronage, hoping they will not condemn this attempt of their sister to be erudite, but rally around me a faithful band of supporters and defenders.

H. E. W.

OUR NIG.

CHAPTER I.

MAG SMITH, MY MOTHER.

Oh, Grief beyond all other griefs, when fate
First leaves the young heart lone and desolate
In the wide world, without that only tie
For which it loved to live or feared to die;
Lorn as the hung-up lute, that ne'er hath spoken
Since the sad day its master-chord was broken!

MOORE.

LONELY MAG SMITH! See her as she walks with downcast eyes and heavy heart. It was not always thus. She *had* a loving, trusting heart. Early deprived of parental guardianship, far removed from relatives, she was left to guide her tiny boat over life's surges alone and inexperienced. As she merged into womanhood, unprotected, uncherished, uncared for, there fell on her ear the music of love, awakening an intensity of emotion long dormant. It whispered of an elevation before unaspired to; of ease and plenty her simple heart had never dreamed of as hers. She knew the voice of her charmer, so ravishing, sounded far above her. It seemed like an angel's, alluring her upward and onward. She thought she could ascend to him and become an equal. She surrendered to him a priceless gem, which he proudly garnered as a trophy, with those of other victims, and left her to her fate. The world seemed full of hateful deceivers and crushing arrogance. Conscious that the great bond of union to her former companions was severed, that the disdain of others would be insupportable, she determined to leave the few friends she possessed, and seek an asylum among strangers. Her offspring came unwelcomed, and before its nativity numbered weeks, it passed from earth, ascending to a purer and better life.

"God be thanked," ejaculated Mag, as she saw its breathing cease; "no one can taunt *her* with my ruin."

Blessed release! may we all respond. How many pure, innocent children not only inherit a wicked heart of their own, claiming life-long scrutiny and restraint, but are heirs also of parental disgrace and calumny, from which only

long years of patient endurance in paths of recti-
tude can disencumber them.

Mag's new home was soon contaminated by
the publicity of her fall; she had a feeling of
degradation oppressing her; but she resolved to
be circumspect, and try to regain in a measure
what she had lost. Then some foul tongue would
jest of her shame, and averted looks and cold
greetings disheartened her. She saw she could
not bury in forgetfulness her misdeed, so she
resolved to leave her home and seek another in
the place she at first fled from.

Alas, how fearful are we to be first in extending a helping hand to those who stagger in the
mires of infamy; to speak the first words of hope
and warning to those emerging into the sunlight
of morality! Who can tell what numbers, ad-
vancing just far enough to hear a cold welcome
and join in the reserved converse of professed
reformers, disappointed, disheartened, have cho-
sen to dwell in unclean places, rather than encounter these "holier-than-thou" of the great
brotherhood of man!

Such was Mag's experience; and disdaining to
ask favor or friendship from a sneering world,

she resolved to shut herself up in a hovel she
had often passed in better days, and which she
knew to be untenanted. She vowed to ask no
favors of familiar faces; to die neglected and forgotten before she would be dependent on any.
Removed from the village, she was seldom seen
except as upon your introduction, gentle reader,
with downcast visage, returning her work to her
employer, and thus providing herself with the
means of subsistence. In two years many hands
craved the same avocation; foreigners who
cheapened toil and clamored for a livelihood,
competed with her, and she could not thus sustain herself. She was now above no drudgery.
Occasionally old acquaintances called to be favored with help of some kind, which she was glad
to bestow for the sake of the money it would
bring her; but the association with them was
such a painful reminder of by-gones, she returned to her hut morose and revengeful, re-
fusing all offers of a better home than she possessed. Thus she lived for years, hugging her
wrongs, but making no effort to escape. She
had never known plenty, scarcely competency;
but the present was beyond comparison with

those innocent years when the coronet of virtue was hers.

Every year her melancholy increased, her means diminished. At last no one seemed to notice her, save a kind-hearted African, who often called to inquire after her health and to see if she needed any fuel, he having the responsibility of furnishing that article, and she in return mending or making garments.

"How much you earn dis week, Mag?" asked he one Saturday evening.

"Little enough, Jim. Two or three days without any dinner. I washed for the Reeds, and did a small job for Mrs. Bellmont; that's all. I shall starve soon, unless I can get more to do. Folks seem as afraid to come here as if they expected to get some awful disease. I do n't believe there is a person in the world but would be glad to have me dead and out of the way."

"No, no, Mag! do n't talk so. You shan't starve so long as I have barrels to hoop. Peter Greene boards me cheap. I'll help you, if nobody else will."

A tear stood in Mag's faded eye. "I'm glad," she said, with a softer tone than before, "if there is *one* who is n't glad to see me suffer. I b'lieve all Singleton wants to see me punished, and feel as if they could tell when I 've been punished long enough. It 's a long day ahead they 'll set it, I reckon."

After the usual supply of fuel was prepared, Jim returned home. Full of pity for Mag, he set about devising measures for her relief. "By golly!" said he to himself one day—for he had become so absorbed in Mag's interest that he had fallen into a habit of musing aloud—"By golly! I wish she 'd *marry* me."

"Who?" shouted Pete Greene, suddenly starting from an unobserved corner of the rude shop.

"Where you come from, you sly nigger!" exclaimed Jim.

"Come, tell me, who is 't?" said Pete; "Mag Smith, you want to marry?"

"Git out, Pete! and when you come in dis shop again, let a nigger know it. Do n't steal in like a thief."

Pity and love know little severance. One attends the other. Jim acknowledged the presence of the former, and his efforts in Mag's behalf told also of a finer principle.

This sudden expedient which he had uninten
tionally disclosed, roused his thinking and invent-
ive powers to study upon the best method of
introducing the subject to Mag.

He belted his barrels, with many a scheme revolving in his mind, none of which quite satisfied
him, or seemed, on the whole, expedient. He
thought of the pleasing contrast between her fair
face and his own dark skin; the smooth, straight
hair, which he had once, in expression of pity,
kindly stroked on her now wrinkled but once
fair brow. There was a tempest gathering in his
heart, and at last, to ease his pent-up passion, he
exclaimed aloud, "By golly!" Recollecting his
former exposure, he glanced around to see if
Pete was in hearing again. Satisfied on this
point, he continued: "She'd be as much of a prize
to me as she'd fall short of coming up to the
mark with white folks. I do n't care for past
things. I 've done things 'fore now I 's 'shamed
of. She 's good enough for me, any how."

One more glance about the premises to be sure
Pete was away.

The next Saturday night brought Jim to the
hovel again. The cold was fast coming to tarry

its apportioned time.   Mag was nearly despairing
of meeting its rigor.

"How's the wood, Mag?" asked Jim.

"All gone; and no more to cut, any how," was
the reply.

"Too bad!" Jim said.   His truthful reply
would have been, I'm glad.

"Anything to eat in the house?" continued he.

"No," replied Mag.

"Too bad!" again, orally, with the same *inward* gratulation as before.

"Well, Mag," said Jim, after a short pause,
"you's down low enough.   I do n't see but I've
got to take care of ye.   'Sposin' we marry!"

Mag raised her eyes, full of amazement, and
uttered a sonorous "What?"

Jim felt abashed for a moment.   He knew well
what were her objections.

"You's had trial of white folks, any how.   They
run off and left ye, and now none of 'em come
near ye to see if you's dead or alive.   I's black
outside, I know, but I's got a white heart inside.
Which you rather have, a black heart in a white
skin, or a white heart in a black one?"

"Oh, dear!" sighed Mag; "Nobody on earth cares for *me* — "

"I do," interrupted Jim.

"I can do but two things," said she, "beg my living, or get it from you."

"Take me, Mag. I can give you a better home than this, and not let you suffer so."

He prevailed; they married. You can philosophize, gentle reader, upon the impropriety of such unions, and preach dozens of sermons on the evils of amalgamation. Want is a more powerful philosopher and preacher. Poor Mag. She has sundered another bond which held her to her fellows. She has descended another step down the ladder of infamy.

CHAPTER II.

MY FATHER'S DEATH.

Misery ! we have known each other,
Like a sister and a brother,
Living in the same lone home
Many years — we must live some
Hours or ages yet to come.

SHELLEY.

JIM, proud of his treasure, — a white wife, — tried hard to fulfil his promises ; and furnished her with a more comfortable dwelling, diet, and apparel. It was comparatively a comfortable winter she passed after her marriage. When Jim could work, all went on well. Industrious, and fond of Mag, he was determined she should not regret her union to him. Time levied an additional charge upon him, in the form of two pretty mulattos, whose infantile pranks amply repaid the additional toil. A few years, and a severe cough and pain in his side compelled him to be an idler for weeks together, and Mag had thus a reminder of by-gones. She cared for him only as a means to subserve her own comfort; yet she nursed him faithfully and true to marriage vows till death released her. He became the victim of consumption. He loved Mag to the last. So long as life continued, he stifled his sensibility to pain, and toiled for her sustenance long after he was able to do so.

A few expressive wishes for her welfare; a hope of better days for her; an anxiety lest they should not all go to the " good place;" brief advice about their children; a hope expressed that Mag would not be neglected as she used to be; the manifestation of Christian patience; these were *all* the legacy of miserable Mag. A feeling of cold desolation came over her, as she turned from the grave of one who had been truly faithful to her.

She was now expelled from companionship with white people; this last step — her union with a black — was the climax of repulsion.

Seth Shipley, a partner in Jim's business, wished her to remain in her present home; but she declined, and returned to her hovel again, with obstacles threefold more iusurmountable than before. Seth accompanied her, giving her a weekly allowance which furnished most of the food necessary for the four inmates. After a time, work failed; their means were reduced.

How Mag toiled and suffered, yielding to fits of desperation, bursts of anger, and uttering curses too fearful to repeat. When both were supplied with work, they prospered; if idle, they were hungry together. In this way their interests became united; they planned for the future together. Mag had lived an outcast for years. She had ceased to feel the gushings of penitence; she had crushed the sharp agonies of an awakened conscience. She had no longings for a purer heart, a better life. Far easier to descend lower. She entered the darkness of perpetual infamy. She asked not the rite of civilization or Christianity. Her will made her the wife of Seth. Soon followed scenes familiar and trying.

" It 's no use," said Seth one day; " we must give the children away, and try to get work in some other place."

" Who 'll take the black devils?" snarled Mag.

"They're none of mine," said Seth; "what you growling about?"

"Nobody will want any thing of mine, or yours either," she replied.

"We'll make 'em, p'r'aps," he said. "There's Frado's six years old, and pretty, if she is yours, and white folks 'll say so. She'd be a prize somewhere," he continued, tipping his chair back against the wall, and placing his feet upon the rounds, as if he had much more to say when in the right position.

Frado, as they called one of Mag's children, was a beautiful mulatto, with long, curly black hair, and handsome, roguish eyes, sparkling with an exuberance of spirit almost beyond restraint.

Hearing her name mentioned, she looked up from her play, to see what Seth had to say of her.

"Wouldn't the Bellmonts take her?" asked Seth.

"Bellmonts?" shouted Mag. "His wife is a right she-devil! and if—"

"Hadn't they better be all together?" inter-

rupted Seth, reminding her of a like epithet
used in reference to her little ones.

Without seeming to notice him, she continued,
"She can't keep a girl in the house over a
week; and Mr. Bellmont wants to hire a boy to
work for him, but he can't find one that will
live in the house with her; she's so ugly, they
can't."

"Well, we've got to make a move soon,"
answered Seth; "if you go with me, we shall go
right off. Had you rather spare the other
one?" asked Seth, after a short pause.

"One's as bad as t'other," replied Mag.
"Frado is such a wild, frolicky thing, and means
to do jest as she's a mind to; she wo n't go if
she do n't want to. I do n't want to tell her
she is to be given away."

"I will," said Seth. "Come here, Frado?"

The child seemed to have some dim fore-
shadowing of evil, and declined.

"Come here," he continued; "I want to tell
you something."

She came reluctantly. He took her hand and
said: "We're going to move, by-'m-bye; will
you go?"

"No!" screamed she; and giving a sudden jerk which destroyed Seth's equilibrium, left him sprawling on the floor, while she escaped through the open door.

"She's a hard one," said Seth, brushing his patched coat sleeve. "I'd risk her at Bellmont's."

They discussed the expediency of a speedy departure. Seth would first seek employment, and then return for Mag. They would take with them what they could carry, and leave the rest with Pete Greene, and come for them when they were wanted. They were long in arranging affairs satisfactorily, and were not a little startled at the close of their conference to find Frado missing. They thought approaching night would bring her. Twilight passed into darkness, and she did not come. They thought she had understood their plans, and had, perhaps, permanently withdrawn. They could not rest without making some effort to ascertain her retreat. Seth went in pursuit, and returned without her. They rallied others when they discovered that another little colored girl was missing, a favorite playmate of Frado's. All effort

proved unavailing. Mag felt sure her fears
were realized, and that she might never see her
again. Before her anxieties became realities,
both were safely returned, and from them and
their attendant they learned that they went to
walk, and not minding the direction soon found
themselves lost. They had climbed fences and
walls, passed through thickets and marshes, and
when night approached selected a thick cluster
of shrubbery as a covert for the night. They
were discovered by the person who now restored
them, chatting of their prospects, Frado attempting to banish the childish fears of her companion. As they were some miles from home,
they were kindly cared for until morning. Mag
was relieved to know her child was not driven
to desperation by their intentions to relieve
themselves of her, and she was inclined to think
severe restraint would be healthful.

The removal was all arranged; the few days
necessary for such migrations passed quickly,
and one bright summer morning they bade farewell to their Singleton hovel, and with budgets
and bundles commenced their weary march.
As they neared the village, they heard the

merry shouts of children gathered around the
schoolroom, awaiting the coming of their teacher.

"Halloo!" screamed one, "Black, white and
yeller!" "Black, white and yeller," echoed a
dozen voices.

It did not grate so harshly on poor Mag as
once it would. She did not even turn her head
to look at them. She had passed into an insen-
sibility no childish taunt could penetrate, else
she would have reproached herself as she passed
familiar scenes, for extending the separation
once so easily annihilated by steadfast integrity.
Two miles beyond lived the Bellmonts, in a
large, old fashioned, two-story white house, en-
vironed by fruitful acres, and embellished by
shrubbery and shade trees. Years ago a youthful couple consecrated it as home; and after
many little feet had worn paths to favorite fruit
trees, and over its green hills, and mingled at
last with brother man in the race which belongs
neither to the swift or strong, the sire became
grey-haired and decrepid, and went to his last
repose. His aged consort soon followed him.
The old homestead thus passed into the hands
of a son, to whose wife Mag had applied the

epithet " she-devil," as may be remembered.
John, the son, had not in his family arrangements departed from the example of the father.
The pastimes of his boyhood were ever freshly
revived by witnessing the games of his own sons
as they rallied about the same goal his youthful
feet had often won; as well as by the amuse-
ments of his daughters in their imitations of
maternal duties.

At the time we introduce them, however,
John is wearing the badge of age. Most of his
children were from home; some seeking employment; some were already settled in homes
of their own. A maiden sister shared with him
the estate on which he resided, and occupied a
portion of the house.

Within sight of the house, Seth seated himself
with his bundles and the child he had been leading, while Mag walked onward to the house
leading Frado. A knock at the door brought
Mrs. Bellmont, and Mag asked if she would be
willing to let that child stop there while she
went to the Reed's house to wash, and when she
came back she would call and get her. It
seemed a novel request, but she consented.

Why the impetuous child entered the house, we cannot tell ; the door closed, and Mag hastily departed. Frado waited for the close of day, which was to bring back her mother. Alas! it never came. It was the last time she ever saw or heard of her mother.

CHAPTER III.

A NEW HOME FOR ME.

Oh! did we but know of the shadows so nigh,
  The world would indeed be a prison of gloom;
All light would be quenched in youth's eloquent eye,
  And the prayer-lisping infant would ask for the tomb.

For if Hope be a star that may lead us astray,
  And "deceiveth the heart," as the aged ones preach;
Yet 'twas Mercy that gave it, to beacon our way,
  Though its halo illumes where it never can reach.

ELIZA COOK.

As the day closed and Mag did not appear,
surmises were expressed by the family that she
never intended to return. Mr. Bellmont was a
kind, humane man, who would not grudge hospi-
tality to the poorest wanderer, nor fail to sympathize with any sufferer, however humble.
The child's desertion by her mother appealed to
his symathy, and he felt inclined to succor her.
To do this in opposition to Mrs. Bellmont's
wishes, would be like encountering a whirlwind

charged with fire, daggers and spikes. She was not as susceptible of fine emotions as her spouse. Mag's opinion of her was not without foundation. She was self-willed, haughty, undisciplined, arbitrary and severe. In common parlance, she was a *scold*, a thorough one. Mr. B. remained silent during the consultation which follows, engaged in by mother, Mary and John, or Jack, as he was familiarly called.

"Send her to the County House," said Mary, in reply to the query what should be done with her, in a tone which indicated self-importance in the speaker. She was indeed the idol of her mother, and more nearly resembled her in disposition and manners than the others.

Jane, an invalid daughter, the eldest of those at home, was reclining on a sofa apparently uninterested.

"Keep her," said Jack. "She's real handsome and bright, and not very black, either."

"Yes," rejoined Mary; "that's just like you, Jack. She'll be of no use at all these three years, right under foot all the time."

"Poh! Miss Mary; if she should stay, it would n't be two days before you would be tell-ing the girls about *our* nig, *our* nig!" retorted Jack.

"I do n't want a nigger 'round *me*, do you, mother?" asked Mary.

"I do n't mind the nigger in the child. I should like a dozen better than one," replied her mother. "If I could make her do my work in a few years, I would keep her. I have so much trouble with girls I hire, I am almost persuaded if I have one to train up in my way from a child, I shall be able to keep them awhile. I am tired of changing every few months."

"Where could she sleep?" asked Mary. "I do n't want her near me."

"In the L chamber," answered the mother.

"How 'll she get there?" asked Jack. "She'll be afraid to go through that dark passage, and she can't climb the ladder safely."

"She 'll have to go there; it 's good enough for a nigger," was the reply.

Jack was sent on horseback to ascertain if Mag was at her home. He returned with the testimony of Pete Greene that they were fairly departed, and that the child was intentionally thrust upon their family.

The imposition was not at all relished by Mrs. B., or the pert, haughty Mary, who had just glided into her teens.

"Show the child to bed, Jack," said his mother. "You seem most pleased with the little nigger, so you may introduce her to her room."

He went to the kitchen, and, taking Frado gently by the hand, told her he would put her in bed now; perhaps her mother would come the next night after her.

It was not yet quite dark, so they ascended the stairs without any light, passing through nicely furnished rooms, which were a source of great amazement to the child. He opened the door which connected with her room by a dark, unfinished passage-way. "Don't bump your head," said Jack, and stepped before to open the door leading into her apartment,— an unfinished chamber over the kitchen, the roof slanting nearly to the floor, so that the bed could stand only in the middle of the room. A small half window furnished light and air. Jack returned to the sitting room with the remark that the child would soon outgrow those quarters.

"When she *does*, she'll outgrow the house," remarked the mother.

"What can she do to help you?" asked Mary. "She came just in the right time, did n't she? Just the very day after Bridget left," continued she.

"I'll see what she can do in the morning," was the answer.

While this conversation was passing below, Frado lay, revolving in her little mind whether she would remain or not until her mother's return. She was of wilful, determined nature, a stranger to fear, and would not hesitate to wander away should she decide to. She remembered the conversation of her mother with Seth, the words "given away" which she heard used in reference to herself; and though she did not know their full import, she thought she should, by remaining, be in some relation to white people she was never favored with before. So she resolved to tarry, with the hope that mother would come and get her some time. The hot sun had penetrated her room, and it was long before a cooling breeze reduced the temperature so that she could sleep.

Frado was called early in the morning by her new mistress. Her first work was to feed the hens. She was shown how it was *always* to be done, and in no other way; any departure from this rule to be punished by a whipping. She was then accompanied by Jack to drive the cows to pasture, so she might learn the way. Upon her return she was allowed to eat her breakfast, consisting of a bowl of skimmed milk, with brown bread crusts, which she was told to eat, standing, by the kitchen table, and must not be over ten minutes about it. Meanwhile the family were taking their morning meal in the dining-room. This over, she was placed on a cricket to wash the common dishes; she was to be in waiting always to bring wood and chips, to run hither and thither from room to room.

A large amount of dish-washing for small hands followed dinner. Then the same after tea and going after the cows finished her first day's work. It was a new discipline to the child. She found some attractions about the place, and she retired to rest at night more willing to remain. The same routine followed day after day, with slight variation; adding a little more work, and spicing the toil with "words that burn," and frequent blows on her head. These were great annoyances to Frado, and had she known where her mother was, she would have gone at once to her. She was often greatly wearied, and silently wept over her sad fate. At first she wept aloud, which Mrs. Bellmont noticed by applying a rawhide, always at hand in the kitchen. It was a symptom of discontent and complaining which must be "nipped in the bud," she said.

Thus passed a year. No intelligence of Mag. It was now certain Frado was to become a permanent member of the family. Her labors were multiplied; she was quite indispensable, although but seven years old. She had never learned to read, never heard of a school until her residence in the family.

Mrs. Bellmont was in doubt about the utility of attempting to educate people of color, who were incapable of elevation. This subject occasioned a lengthy discussion in the family. Mr. Bellmont, Jane and Jack arguing for Frado's education; Mary and her mother objecting. At last Mr. Bellmont declared decisively that she *should* go to school. He was a man who seldom

decided controversies at home. The word once
spoken admitted of no appeal; so, notwithstand-
ing Mary's objection that she would have to
attend the same school she did, the word became
law.

It was to be a new scene to Frado, and Jack
had many queries and conjectures to answer.
He was himself too far advanced to attend the
summer school, which Frado regretted, having
had too many opportunities of witnessing Miss
Mary's temper to feel safe in her company alone.

The opening day of school came. Frado
sauntered on far in the rear of Mary, who was
ashamed to be seen "walking with a nigger."
As soon as she appeared, with scanty clothing
and bared feet, the children assembled, noisily
published her approach: "See that nigger,"
shouted one. "Look! look!" cried another.
"I won't play with her," said one little girl.
"Nor I neither," replied another.

Mary evidently relished these sharp attacks,
and saw a fair prospect of lowering Nig where,
according to her views, she belonged. Poor
Frado, chagrined and grieved, felt that her an-
ticipations of pleasure at such a place were far

from being realized. She was just deciding
to return home, and never come there again,
when the teacher appeared, and observing the
downcast looks of the child, took her by the
hand, and led her into the school-room. All followed, and, after the bustle of securing seats
was over, Miss Marsh inquired if the children
knew "any cause for the sorrow of that little
girl?" pointing to Frado. It was soon all told.
She then reminded them of their duties to the
poor and friendless; their cowardice in attack-
ing a young innocent child; referred them to
one who looks not on outward appearances, but
on the heart. "She looks like a good girl; I
think *I* shall love her, so lay aside all prejudice,
and vie with each other in shewing kindness
and good-will to one who seems different from
you," were the closing remarks of the kind lady.
Those kind words! The most agreeable sound
which ever meets the ear of sorrowing, griev-
ing childhood.

Example rendered her words efficacious. Day
by day there was a manifest change of de-
portment towards "Nig." Her speeches often
drew merriment from the children; no one

could do more to enliven their favorite pastimes
than Frado.   Mary could not endure to see her
thus noticed, yet knew not how to prevent it.
She could not influence her schoolmates as she
wished.   She had not gained their affections
by winning ways and yielding points of con-
troversy.   On the contrary, she was self-willed,
domineering; every day reported "mad" by
some of her companions.   She availed herself
of the only alternative, abuse and taunts, as
they returned from school.   This was not satis-
factory; she wanted to use physical force "to
subdue her," to "keep her down."

There was, on their way home, a field inter-
sected by a stream over which a single plank
was placed for a crossing.   It occurred to Mary that it would be a punishment to Nig to
compel her to cross over; so she dragged her
to the edge, and told her authoritatively to go
over.   Nig hesitated, resisted.   Mary placed
herself behind the child, and, in the struggle
to force her over, lost her footing and plunged
into the stream.   Some of the larger scholars
being in sight, ran, and thus prevented Mary
from drowning and Frado from falling.   Nig

scampered home fast as possible, and Mary went
to the nearest house, dripping, to procure a
change of garments. She came loitering home,
half crying, exclaiming, "Nig pushed me into
the stream!" She then related the particulars.
Nig was called from the kitchen. Mary stood
with anger flashing in her eyes. Mr. Bellmont
sat quietly reading his paper. He had wit-
nessed too many of Miss Mary's outbreaks to
be startled. Mrs. Bellmont interrogated Nig.

"I did n't do it! I did n't do it!" answered
Nig, passionately, and then related the occurrence truthfully.

The discrepancy greatly enraged Mrs. Bellmont. With loud accusations and angry ges-
tures she approached the child. Turning to
her husband, she asked,

"Will you sit still, there, and hear that
black nigger call Mary a liar?"

"How do we know but she has told
the truth? I shall not punish her," he replied, and left the house, as he usually did
when a tempest threatened to envelop him.
No sooner was he out of sight than Mrs. B.
and Mary commenced beating her inhumanly;

then propping her mouth open with a piece
of wood, shut her up in a dark room, without any supper. For employment, while the
tempest raged within, Mr. Bellmont went for
the cows, a task belonging to Frado, and thus
unintentionally prolonged her pain. At dark
Jack came in, and seeing Mary, accosted her
with, "So you thought you'd vent your spite
on Nig, did you? Why can't you let her
alone? It was good enough for you to get
a ducking, only you did not stay in half long
enough."

"Stop!" said his mother. "You shall never
talk so before me. You would have that little
nigger trample on Mary, would you? She
came home with a lie; it made Mary's story
false."

"What was Mary's story?" asked Jack.

It was related.

"Now," said Jack, sallying into a chair, "the
school-children happened to see it all, and they
tell the same story Nig does. Which is most
likely to be true, what a dozen agree they
saw, or the contrary?"

"It is very strange you will believe what

others say against your sister," retorted his
mother, with flashing eye. "I think it is time
your father subdued you."

"Father is a sensible man," argued Jack.
"He would not wrong a dog. Where *is* Frado?" he continued.

"Mother gave her a good whipping and
shut her up," replied Mary.

Just then Mr. Bellmont entered, and asked if
Frado was "shut up yet."

The knowledge of her innocence, the perfidy
of his sister, worked fearfully on Jack. He
bounded from his chair, searched every room
till he found the child; her mouth wedged
apart, her face swollen, and full of pain.

How Jack pitied her! He relieved her jaws,
brought her some supper, took her to her room,
comforted her as well as he knew how, sat by her
till she fell asleep, and then left for the sitting
room. As he passed his mother, he remarked,
"If that was the way Frado was to be treated, he
hoped she would never wake again!" He then
imparted her situation to his father, who seemed
untouched, till a glance at Jack exposed a tearful eye. Jack went early to her next morning.

She awoke sad, but refreshed. After breakfast Jack took her with him to the field, and kept her through the day. But it could not be so generally. She must return to school, to her household duties. He resolved to do what he could to protect her from Mary and his mother. He bought her a dog, which became a great favorite with both. The invalid, Jane, would gladly befriend her; but she had not the strength to brave the iron will of her mother. Kind words and affectionate glances were the only expressions of sympathy she could safely indulge in. The men employed on the farm were always glad to hear her prattle; she was a great favorite with them. Mrs. Bellmont allowed them the privilege of talking with her in the kitchen. She did not fear but she should have ample opportunity of subduing her when they were away. Three months of schooling, summer and winter, she enjoyed for three years. Her winter over-dress was a cast-off overcoat, once worn by Jack, and a sun-bonnet. It was a source of great merriment to the scholars, but Nig's retorts were so mirthful, and their satisfaction so evident in attributing the selection to

" Old Granny Bellmont," that it was not painful
to Nig or pleasurable to Mary. Her jollity was
not to be quenched by whipping or scolding.
In Mrs. Bellmont's presence she was under restraint; but in the kitchen, and among her
schoolmates, the pent up fires burst forth. She
was ever at some sly prank when unseen by her
teacher, in school hours; not unfrequently some
outburst of merriment, of which she was the
original, was charged upon some innocent mate,
and punishment inflicted which she merited.
They enjoyed her antics so fully that any of
them would suffer wrongfully to keep open the
avenues of mirth. She would venture far beyond propriety, thus shielded and countenanced.

The teacher's desk was supplied with drawers,
in which were stored his books and other *et
ceteras* of the profession. The children observed
Nig very busy there one morning before school,
as they flitted in occasionally from their play
outside. The master came; called the children
to order; opened a drawer to take the book the
occasion required; when out poured a volume of
smoke. " Fire ! fire !" screamed he, at the top of
his voice. By this time he had become suf-

ficiently acquainted with the peculiar odor, to know he was imposed upon. The scholars shouted with laughter to see the terror of the dupe, who, feeling abashed at the needless fright, made no very strict investigation, and Nig once more escaped punishment. She had provided herself with cigars, and puffing, puffing away at the crack of the drawer, had filled it with smoke, and then closed it tightly to deceive the teacher, and amuse the scholars. The interim of terms was filled up with a variety of duties new and peculiar. At home, no matter how powerful the heat when sent to rake hay or guard the grazing herd, she was never permitted to shield her skin from the sun. She was not many shades darker than Mary now; what a calamity it would be ever to hear the contrast spoken of. Mrs. Bellmont was determined the sun should have full power to darken the shade which nature had first bestowed upon her as best befitting.

CHAPTER IV.

A FRIEND FOR NIG.

"Hours of my youth! when nurtured in my breast,
To love a stranger, friendship made me blest; —
Friendship, the dear peculiar bond of youth,
When every artless bosom throbs with truth;
Untaught by worldly wisdom how to feign;
And check each impulse with prudential reign;
When all we feel our honest souls disclose —
In love to friends, in open hate to foes;
No varnished tales the lips of youth repeat,
No dear-bought knowledge purchased by deceit."

BYRON.

WITH what differing emotions have the denizens of earth awaited the approach of to-day.
Some sufferer has counted the vibrations of the
pendulum impatient for its dawn, who, now that
it has arrived, is anxious for its close. The votary of pleasure, conscious of yesterday's void,
wishes for power to arrest time's haste till a few
more hours of mirth shall be enjoyed. The unfortunate are yet gazing in vain for golden-edged clouds they fancied would appear in their
horizon. The good man feels that he has accom-

plished too little for the Master, and sighs that
another day must so soon close. Innocent childhood, weary of its stay, longs for another mor-
row; busy manhood cries, hold! hold! and pur-
sues it to another's dawn. All are dissatisfied.
All crave some good not yet possessed, which
time is expected to bring with all its morrows.

Was it strange that, to a disconsolate child,
three years should seem a long, long time?
During school time she had rest from Mrs. Bellmont's tyranny. She was now nine years old;
time, her mistress said, such privileges should
cease.

She could now read and spell, and knew the
elementary steps in grammar, arithmetic, and
writing. Her education completed, as *she* said, Mrs.
Bellmont felt that her time and person belonged
solely to her. She was under her in every sense
of the word. What an opportunity to indulge
her vixen nature ! No matter what occurred to
ruffle her, or from what source provocation came,
real or fancied, a few blows on Nig seemed to
relieve her of a portion of ill-will.

These were days when Fido was the entire
confidant of Frado. She told him her griefs as

though he were human; and he sat so still, and listened so attentively, she really believed he knew her sorrows. All the leisure moments she could gain were used in teaching him some feat of dog-agility, so that Jack pronounced him very knowing, and was truly gratified to know he had furnished her with a gift answering his intentions.

Fido was the constant attendant of Frado, when sent from the house on errands, going and returning with the cows, out in the fields, to the village. If ever she forgot her hardships it was in his company.

Spring was now retiring. James, one of the absent sons, was expected home on a visit. He had never seen the last acquisition to the family. Jack had written faithfully of all the merits of his colored *protegé*, and hinted plainly that mother did not always treat her just right. Many were the preparations to make the visit pleasant, and as the day approached when he was to arrive, great exertions were made to cook the favorite viands, to prepare the choicest table-fare.

The morning of the arrival day was a busy

one. Frado knew not who would be of so much importance; her feet were speeding hither and thither so unsparingly. Mrs. Bellmont seemed a trifle fatigued, and her shoes which had, early in the morning, a methodic squeak, altered to an irregular, peevish snap.

"Get some little wood to make the fire burn," said Mrs. Bellmont, in a sharp tone. Frado obeyed, bringing the smallest she could find.

Mrs. Bellmont approached her, and, giving her a box on her ear, reiterated the command.

The first the child brought was the smallest to be found; of course, the second must be a trifle larger. She well knew it was, as she threw it into a box on the hearth. To Mrs. Bellmont it was a greater affront, as well as larger wood, so she "taught her" with the raw-hide, and sent her the third time for "little wood."

Nig, weeping, knew not what to do. She had carried the smallest; none left would suit her mistress; of course further punishment awaited her; so she gathered up whatever came first, and threw it down on the hearth. As she expected, Mrs. Bellmont, enraged, approached her, and kicked her so forcibly as to throw her upon the floor. Before she could rise, another foiled the attempt, and then followed kick after kick in quick succession and power, till she reached the door. Mr. Bellmont and Anut Abby, hearing the noise, rushed in, just in time to see the last of the performance. Nig jumped up, and rushed from the house, out of sight.

Aunt Abby returned to her apartment, followed by John, who was muttering to himself.

"What were you saying?" asked Aunt Abby.

"I said I hoped the child never would come into the house again."

"What would become of her? You cannot mean *that*," continued his sister.

"I do mean it. The child does as much work as a woman ought to; and just see how she is kicked about!"

"Why do you have it so, John?" asked his sister.

"How am I to help it? Women rule the earth, and all in it."

"I think I should rule my own house, John,"—

"And live in hell meantime," added Mr. Bellmont.

John now sauntered out to the barn to await the quieting of the storm.

Aunt Abby had a glimpse of Nig as she passed out of the yard; but to arrest her, or shew her that *she* would shelter her, in Mrs. Bellmont's presence, would only bring reserved wrath on her defenceless head. Her sister-in-law had great prejudices against her. One cause of the alienation was that she did not give her right in the homestead to John, and leave it forever; another was that she was a professor of religion, (so was Mrs. Bellmont;) but Nab, as she called her, did not live according to her profession; another, that she *would* sometimes give Nig cake and pie, which she was never allowed to have at home. Mary had often noticed and spoken of her inconsistencies.

The dinner hour passed. Frado had not appeared. Mrs. B. made no inquiry or search. Aunt Abby looked long, and found her concealed in an outbuilding. "Come into the house with me," implored Aunt Abby.

"I ain't going in any more," sobbed the child.

"What will you do?" asked Aunt Abby.

"I've got to stay out here and die. I ha'n't got no mother, no home. I wish I was dead."

"Poor thing," muttered Aunt Abby; and slyly providing her with some dinner, left her to her grief.

Jane went to confer with her Aunt about the affair; and learned from her the retreat. She would gladly have concealed her in her own chamber, and ministered to her wants; but she was dependent on Mary and her mother for care, and any displeasure caused by attention to Nig, was seriously felt.

Toward night the coach brought James. A time of general greeting, inquiries for absent members of the family, a visit to Aunt Abby's room, undoing a few delicacies for Jane, brought them to the tea hour.

"Where's Frado?" asked Mr. Bellmont, observing she was not in her usual place, behind her mistress' chair.

"I don't know, and I don't care. If she makes her appearance again, I'll take the skin from her body," replied his wife.

James, a fine looking young man, with a pleasant countenance, placid, and yet decidedly

serious, yet not stern, looked up confounded.
He was no stranger to his mother's nature; but
years of absence had erased the occurrences
once so familiar, and he asked, "Is this that
pretty little Nig, Jack writes to me about, that
you are so severe upon, mother?"

"I'll not leave much of her beauty to be
seen, if she comes in sight; and now, John,"
said Mrs, B., turning to her husband, "you need
not think you are going to learn her to treat me
in this way; just see how saucy she was this
morning. She shall learn her place."

Mr. Bellmont raised his calm, determined eye
full upon her, and said, in a decisive manner:
"You shall not strike, or scald, or skin her, as you
call it, if she comes back again. Remember!"
and he brought his hand down upon the table.
"I have searched an hour for her now, and she
is not to be found on the premises. Do *you*
know where she is? Is she *your* prisoner?"

"No! I have just told you I did not know
where she was. Nab has her hid somewhere, I
suppose. Oh, dear! I did not think it would
come to this; that my own husband would treat
me so." Then came fast flowing tears, which no

one but Mary seemed to notice. Jane crept
into Aunt Abby's room; Mr. Bellmont and
James went out of doors, and Mary remained to
condole with her parent.

"Do you know where Frado is?" asked Jane
of her aunt.

"No," she replied. "I have hunted everywhere. She has left her first hiding-place. I
cannot think what has become of her. There
comes Jack and Fido; perhaps he knows;" and
she walked to a window near, where James and
his father were conversing together.

The two brothers exchanged a hearty greeting, and then Mr. Bellmont told Jack to eat his
supper; afterward he wished to send him away.
He immediately went in. Accustomed to all
the phases of indoor storms, from a whine to
thunder and lightning, he saw at a glance marks
of disturbance. He had been absent through
the day, with the hired men.

"What's the fuss?" asked he, rushing into
Aunt Abby's.

"Eat your supper," said Jane; "go home,
Jack."

Back again through the dining-room, and out to his father.

"What's the fuss?" again inquired he of his father.

"Eat your supper, Jack, and see if you can find Frado. She's not been seen since morning, and then she was kicked out of the house."

"I shan't eat my supper till I find her," said Jack, indignantly. "Come, James, and see the little creature mother treats so."

They started, calling, searching, coaxing, all their way along. No Frado. They returned to the house to consult. James and Jack declared they would not sleep till she was found.

Mrs. Bellmont attempted to dissuade them from the search. "It was a shame a little *nigger* should make so much trouble."

Just then Fido came running up, and Jack exclaimed, "Fido knows where she is, I'll bet."

"So I believe," said his father; "but we shall not be wiser unless we can outwit him. He will not do what his mistress forbids him."

"I know how to fix him," said Jack. Taking a plate from the table, which was still waiting, he called, "Fido! Fido! Frado wants some supper. Come!" Jack started, the dog followed, and soon capered on before, far, far into the fields, over walls and through fences, into a piece of swampy land. Jack followed close, and soon appeared to James, who was quite in the rear, coaxing and forcing Frado along with him.

A frail child, driven from shelter by the cruelty of his mother, was an object of interest to James. They persuaded her to go home with them, warmed her by the kitchen fire, gave her a good supper, and took her with them into the sitting-room.

"Take that nigger out of my sight," was Mrs. Bellmont's command, before they could be seated.

James led her into Aunt Abby's, where he knew they were welcome. They chatted awhile until Frado seemed cheerful; then James led her to her room, and waited until she retired.

"Are you glad I've come home?" asked James.

"Yes; if you won't let me be whipped tomorrow."

"You won't be whipped. You must try to be a good girl," counselled James.

"If I do, I get whipped;" sobbed the child. "They won't believe what I say. Oh, I wish I had my mother back; then I should not be kicked and whipped so. Who made me so?"

"God;" answered James.

"Did God make you?"

"Yes."

"Who made Aunt Abby?"

"God."

"Who made your mother?"

"God."

"Did the same God that made her make me?"

"Yes."

"Well, then, I don't like him."

"Why not?"

"Because he made her white, and me black. Why didn't he make us *both* white?"

"I don't know; try to go to sleep, and you will feel better in the morning," was all the reply he could make to her knotty queries. It was a long time before she fell asleep; and a number of days before James felt in a mood to visit and entertain old associates and friends.

CHAPTER V.

DEPARTURES.

Life is a strange avenue of various trees and flowers;
Lightsome at commencement, but darkening to its end in a distant,
  massy portal.
It beginneth as a little path, edged with the violet and primrose,
A little path of lawny grass and soft to tiny feet.
Soon, spring thistles in the way.

TUPPER.

JAMES' visit concluded. Frado had become
greatly attached to him, and with sorrow she
listened and joined in the farewells which pre-
ceded his exit. The remembrance of his kindness cheered her through many a weary month,
and an occasional word to her in letters to Jack,
were like " cold waters to a thirsty soul." Intelligence came that James would soon marry;
Frado hoped he would, and remove her from
such severe treatment as she was subject to.
There had been additional burdens laid on her
since his return. She must now *milk* the cows,
she had then only to drive. Flocks of sheep
had been added to the farm, which daily claimed

a portion of her time. In the absence of the
men, she must harness the horse for Mary and
her mother to ride, go to mill, in short, do the
work of a boy, could one be procured to endure
the tirades of Mrs. Bellmont. She was first up
in the morning, doing what she could towards
breakfast. Occasionally, she would utter some
funny thing for Jack's benefit, while she was
waiting on the table, provoking a sharp look
from his mother, or expulsion from the room.

On one such occasion, they found her on the
roof of the barn. Some repairs having been
necessary, a staging had been erected, and was
not wholly removed. Availing herself of lad-
ders, she was mounted in high glee on the top-
most board. Mr. Bellmont called sternly for her
to come down; poor Jane nearly fainted from
fear. Mrs. B. and Mary did not care if she
"broke her neck," while Jack and the men
laughed at her fearlessness. Strange, one spark
of playfulness could remain amid such constant
toil; but her natural temperament was in a
high degree mirthful, and the encouragement
she received from Jack and the hired men, constantly nurtured the inclination. When she had

none of the family around to be merry with,
she would amuse herself with the animals.
Among the sheep was a willful leader, who always persisted in being first served, and many
times in his fury he had thrown down Nig, till,
provoked, she resolved to punish him. The pasture in which the sheep grazed was bounded on
three sides by a wide stream, which flowed on
one side at the base of precipitous banks. The
first spare moments at her command, she ran to
the pasture with a dish in her hand, and mount-
ing the highest point of land nearest the stream,
called the flock to their mock repast. Mr Bellmont, with his laborers, were in sight, though
unseen by Frado. They paused to see what she
was about to do. Should she by any mishap
lose her footing, she must roll into the stream,
and, without aid, must drown. They thought of
shouting; but they feared an unexpected salute
might startle her, and thus ensure what they
were anxious to prevent. They watched in
breathless silence. The willful sheep came furi-
ously leaping and bounding far in advance of
the flock. Just as he leaped for the dish, she
suddenly jumped one side, when down he rolled

into the river, and swimming across, remained
alone till night. The men lay down, convulsed
with laughter at the trick, and guessed at once
its object. Mr. Bellmont talked seriously to the
child for exposing herself to such danger; but
she hopped about on her toes, and with laugha-
ble grimaces replied, she knew she was quick
enough to "give him a slide."

But to return. James married a Baltimorean
lady of wealthy parentage, an indispensable
requisite, his mother had always taught him.
He did not marry her wealth, though; he loved
her, sincerely. She was not unlike his sister
Jane, who had a social, gentle, loving nature,
rather *too* yielding, her brother thought. His
Susan had a firmness which Jane needed to
complete her character, but which her ill health
may in a measure have failed to produce. Although an invalid, she was not excluded from
society. Was it strange *she* should seem a desir-
able companion, a treasure as a wife?

Two young men seemed desirous of possess-
ing her. One was a neighbor, Henry Reed, a
tall, spare young man, with sandy hair, and blue,
sinister eyes. He seemed to appreciate her

wants, and watch with interest her improvement
or decay. His kindness she received, and by it
was almost won. Her mother wished her to en-
courage his attentions. She had counted the
acres which were to be transmitted to an only
son; she knew there was silver in the purse;
she would not have Jane too sentimental.

The eagerness with which he amassed wealth,
was repulsive to Jane; he did not spare his person or beasts in its pursuit. She felt that to
such a man she should be considered an incum-
brance; she doubted if he would desire her, if
he did not know she would bring a handsome
patrimony. Her mother, full in favor with the
parents of Henry, commanded her to accept
him. She engaged herself, yielding to her
mother's wishes, because she had not strength to
oppose them; and sometimes, when witness of
her mother's and Mary's tyranny, she felt any
change would be preferable, even such a one as
this. She knew her husband should be the man
of her own selecting, one she was conscious of
preferring before all others. She could not say
this of Henry.

In this dilemma, a visitor came to Aunt

Abby's; one of her boy-favorites, George Means, from an adjoining State. Sensible, plain looking, agreeable, talented, he could not long be a stranger to any one who wished to know him. Jane was accustomed to sit much with Aunt Abby always; her presence now seemed necessary to assist in entertaining this youthful friend. Jane was more pleased with him each day, and silently wished Henry possessed more refinement, and the polished manners of George. She felt dissatisfied with her relation to him. His calls while George was there, brought their opposing qualities vividly before her, and she found it disagreeable to force herself into those attentions belonging to him. She received him apparently only as a neighbor.

George returned home, and Jane endeavored to stifle the risings of dissatisfaction, and had nearly succeeded, when a letter came which needed but one glance to assure her of its birthplace; and she retired for its perusal. Well was it for her that her mother's suspicion was not aroused, or her curiosity startled to inquire who it came from. After reading it, she glided into Aunt Abby's, and placed it in her hands, who was no stranger to Jane's trials.

George could not rest after his return, he
wrote, until he had communicated to Jane the
emotions her presence awakened, and his desire
to love and possess her as his own.   He begged
to know if his affections were reciprocated, or
could be; if she would permit him to write to
her; if she was free from all obligation to
another.

"What would mother say?" queried Jane, as
she received the letter from her aunt.

"Not much to comfort you."

"Now, aunt, George is just such a man as I
could really love, I think, from all I have seen
of him; you know I never could say that of
Henry" —

"Then don't marry him," interrupted Aunt
Abby.

"Mother will make me."

"Your father won't."

"Well, aunt, what can I do?   Would you
answer the letter, or not?"

"Yes, answer it.   Tell him your situation."

"I shall not tell him all my feelings."

Jane answered that she had enjoyed his company much; she had seen nothing offensive in

his manner or appearance; that she was under no obligations which forbade her receiving letters from him as a friend and acquaintance. George was puzzled by the reply. He wrote to Aunt Abby, and from her learned all. He could not see Jane thus sacrificed, without making an effort to rescue her. Another visit followed. George heard Jane say she preferred *him*. He then conferred with Henry at his home. It was not a pleasant subject to talk upon. To be thus supplanted, was not to be thought of. He would sacrifice everything but his inheritance to secure his betrothed.

"And so you are the cause of her late coldness towards me. Leave! I will talk no more about it; the business is settled between us; there it will remain," said Henry.

"Have you no wish to know the real state of Jane's affections towards you?" asked George.

"No! Go, I say! go!" and Henry opened the door for him to pass out.

He retired to Aunt Abby's. Henry soon followed, and presented his cause to Mrs. Bellmont.

Provoked, surprised, indignant, she summoned Jane to her presence, and after a lengthy tirade upon Nab, and her satanic influence, told her she could not break the bonds which held her to Henry; she should not. George Means was rightly named; he was, truly, mean enough; she knew his family of old; his father had four wives, and five times as many children.

"Go to your room, Miss Jane," she continued. "Do n't let me know of your being in Nab's for one while."

The storm was now visible to all beholders. Mr. Bellmont sought Jane. She told him her objections to Henry; showed him George's letter; told her answer, the occasion of his visit. He bade her not make herself sick; he would see that she was not compelled to violate her free choice in so important a transaction. He then sought the two young men; told them he could not as a father see his child compelled to an uncongenial union; a free, voluntary choice was of such importance to one of her health. She must be left free to her own choice.

Jane sent Henry a letter of dismission; he her one of a legal bearing, in which he balanced his disappointment by a few hundreds.

To brave her mother's fury, nearly overcame

her, but the consolations of a kind father and aunt cheered her on. After a suitable interval she was married to George, and removed to his home in Vermont. Thus another light disappeared from Nig's horizon. Another was soon to follow. Jack was anxious to try his skill in providing for his own support; so a situation as clerk in a store was procured in a Western city, and six months after Jane's departure, was Nig abandoned to the tender mercies of Mary and her mother. As if to remove the last vestige of earthly joy, Mrs. Bellmont sold the companion and pet of Frado, the dog Fido.

CHAPTER VI.

VARIETIES.

"Hard are life's early steps; and but that youth is buoyant, confident, and strong in hope, men would behold its threshold and despair."

THE sorrow of Frado was very great for her pet, and Mr. Bellmont by great exertion obtained it again, much to the relief of the child. To be thus deprived of all her sources of pleasure was a sure way to exalt their worth, and Fido became, in her estimation, a more valuable presence than the human beings who surrounded her.

James had now been married a number of years, and frequent requests for a visit from the family were at last accepted, and Mrs. Bellmont made great preparations for a fall sojourn in Baltimore. Mary was installed housekeper — in name merely, for Nig was the only moving power in the house. Although suffering from their joint severity, she felt safer than to be thrown wholly upon an ardent, passionate, unrestrained young lady, whom she always hated and felt it hard to be obliged to obey. The trial she must meet. Were Jack or Jane at home she would have some refuge; one only remained; good Aunt Abby was still in the house.

She saw the fast receding coach which conveyed her master and mistress with regret, and begged for one favor only, that James would send for her when they returned, a hope she had confidently cherished all these five years.

She was now able to do all the washing, ironing, baking, and the common *et cetera* of household duties, though but fourteen. Mary left all for her to do, though she affected great responsibility. She would show herself in the kitchen long enough to relieve herself of some command, better withheld; or insist upon some compliance to her wishes in some department which she was very imperfectly acquainted with, very much less than the person she was addressing; and so impetuous till her orders were obeyed, that to escape the turmoil, Nig would often go contrary to her own knowledge to gain a respite.

Nig was taken sick! What could be done

The *work*, certainly, but not by Miss Mary. So Nig would work while she could remain erect, then sink down upon the floor, or a chair, till she could rally for a fresh effort. Mary would look in upon her, chide her for her laziness, threaten to tell mother when she came home, and so forth.

"Nig!" screamed Mary, one of her sickest days, "come here, and sweep these threads from the carpet." She attempted to drag her weary limbs along, using the broom as support. Impatient of delay, she called again, but with a different request. "Bring me some wood, you lazy jade, quick." Nig rested the broom against the wall, and started on the fresh behest.

Too long gone. Flushed with anger, she rose and greeted her with, "What are you gone so long, for? Bring it in quick, I say."

"I am coming as quick as I can," she replied, entering the door.

"Saucy, impudent nigger, you! is this the way you answer me?" and taking a large carving knife from the table, she hurled it, in her rage, at the defenceless girl.

Dodging quickly, it fastened in the ceiling a

few inches from where she stood. There rushed on Mary's mental vision a picture of bloodshed, in which she was the perpetrator, and the sad consequences of what was so nearly an actual occurrence.

"Tell anybody of this, if you dare. If you tell Aunt Abby, I'll certainly kill you," said she, terrified. She returned to her room, brushed her threads herself; was for a day or two more guarded, and so escaped deserved and merited penalty.

Oh, how long the weeks seemed which held Nig in subjection to Mary; but they passed like all earth's sorrows and joys. Mr. and Mrs. B. returned delighted with their visit, and laden with rich presents for Mary. No word of hope for Nig. James was quite unwell, and would come home the next spring for a visit.

This, thought Nig, will be my time of release. I shall go back with him.

From early dawn until after all were retired, was she toiling, overworked, disheartened, longing for relief.

Exposure from heat to cold, or the reverse, often destroyed her health for short intervals.

She wore no shoes until after frost, and snow even, appeared; and bared her feet again before the last vestige of winter disappeared. These sudden changes she was so illy guarded against, nearly conquered her physical system. Any word of complaint was severely repulsed or cruelly punished.

She was told she had much more than she deserved. So that manual labor was not in reality her only burden; but such an incessant torrent of scolding and boxing and threatening, was enough to deter one of maturer years from remaining within sound of the strife.

It is impossible to give an impression of the manifest enjoyment of Mrs. B. in these kitchen scenes. It was her favorite exercise to enter the appartment noisily, vociferate orders, give a few sudden blows to quicken Nig's pace, then return to the sitting room with *such* a satisfied expression, congratulating herself upon her thorough house-keeping qualities.

She usually rose in the morning at the ringing of the bell for breakfast; if she were heard stirring before that time, Nig knew well there was an extra amount of scolding to be borne.

No one now stood between herself and Frado, but Aunt Abby. And if *she* dared to interfere in the least, she was ordered back to her " own quarters." Nig would creep slyly into her room, learn what she could of her regarding the absent, and thus gain some light in the thick gloom of care and toil and sorrow in which she was immersed.

The first of spring a letter came from James, announcing declining health. He must try northern air as a restorative; so Frado joyfully prepared for this agreeable increase of the family, this addition to her cares.

He arrived feeble, lame, from his disease, so changed Frado wept at his appearance, fearing he would be removed from her forever. He kindly greeted her, took her to the parlor to see his wife and child, and said many things to kindle smiles on her sad face.

Frado felt so happy in his presence, so safe from maltreatment! He was to her a shelter. He observed, silently, the ways of the house a few days; Nig still took her meals in the same manner as formerly, having the same allowance of food.   He, one day, bade her not remove the food, but sit down to the table and eat.

"She *will,* mother," said he, calmly, but impera- tively; I'm determined; she works hard; I've watched her. Now, while I stay, she is going to sit down *here,* and eat such food as we eat."

A few sparks from the mother's black eyes were the only reply; she feared to oppose where she knew she could not prevail. So Nig's stand- ing attitude, and selected diet vanished.

Her clothing was yet poor and scanty; she was not blessed with a Sunday attire; for she was never permitted to attend church with her mis- tress. "Religion was not meant for niggers," *she* said; when the husband and brothers were absent, she would drive Mrs. B. and Mary there, then return, and go for them at the close of the service, but never remain. Aunt Abby would take her to evening meetings, held in the neigh- borhood, which Mrs. B. never attended; and im- part to her lessons of truth and grace as they walked to the place of prayer.

Many of less piety would scorn to present so doleful a figure; Mrs. B. had shaved her glossy ringlets; and, in her coarse cloth gown and ancient bonnet, she was anything but an enticing object. But Aunt Abby looked within. She saw a soul to save, an immortality of happiness to secure.

These evenings were eagerly anticipated by Nig; it was such a pleasant release from labor.

Such perfect contrast in the melody and prayers of these good people to the harsh tones which fell on her ears during the day.

Soon she had all their sacred songs at command, and enlivened her toil by accompanying it with this melody.

James encouraged his aunt in her efforts. He had found the *Saviour*, he wished to have Frado's desolate heart gladdened, quieted, sustained, by *His* presence. He felt sure there were elements in her heart which, transformed and purified by the gospel, would make her worthy the esteem and friendship of the world. A kind, affectionate heart, native wit, and common sense, and the pertness she sometimes exhibited, he felt if restrained properly, might become useful in originating a self-reliance which would be of service to her in after years.

Yet it was not possible to compass all this, while she remained where she was. He wished to be cautious about pressing too closely her claims on his mother, as it would increase the burdened one he so anxiously wished to relieve. He cheered her on with the hope of returning with his family, when he recovered sufficiently.

Nig seemed awakened to new hopes and aspirations, and realized a longing for the future, hitherto unknown.

To complete Nig's enjoyment, Jack arrived unexpectedly. His greeting was as hearty to herself as to any of the family.

"Where are your curls, Fra?" asked Jack, after the usual salutation.

"Your mother cut them off."

"Thought you were getting handsome, did she? Same old story, is it; knocks and bumps? Better times coming; never fear, Nig."

How different this appellative sounded from him; he said it in such a tone, with such a rogueish look!

She laughed, and replied that he had better take her West for a housekeeper.

Jack was pleased with James's innovations of

table discipline, and would often tarry in the dining-room, to see Nig in her new place at the family table. As he was thus sitting one day, after the family had finished dinner, Frado seated herself in her mistress' chair, and was just reaching for a clean dessert plate which was on the table, when her mistress entered.

"Put that plate down; you shall not have a clean one; eat from mine," continued she. Nig hesitated. To eat after James, his wife or Jack, would have been pleasant; but to be command-ed to do what was disagreeable by her mistress, *because* it was disagreeable, was trying. Quickly looking about, she took the plate, called Fido to wash it, which he did to the best of his ability; then, wiping her knife and fork on the cloth, she proceeded to eat her dinner.

Nig never looked toward her mistress during the process. She had Jack near; she did not fear her now.

Insulted, full of rage, Mrs. Bellmont rushed to her husband, and commanded him to notice this insult; to whip that child; if he would not do it, James ought.

James came to hear the kitchen version of the

affair. Jack was boiling over with laughter. He related all the circumstances to James, and pulling a bright, silver half-dollar from his pocket, he threw it at Nig, saying, " There, take that ; 't was worth paying for."

James sought his mother ; told her he " would not excuse or palliate Nig's impudence ; but she should not be whipped or be punished at all. You have not treated her, mother, so as to gain her love ; she is only exhibiting your remissness in this matter."

She only smothered her resentment until a convenient opportunity offered. The first time she was left alone with Nig, she gave her a thorough beating, to bring up arrearages ; and threatened, if she ever exposed her to James, she would " cut her tongue out."

James found her, upon his return, sobbing ; but fearful of revenge, she dared not answer his queries. He guessed their cause, and longed for returning health to take her under his protection.

CHAPTER VII.

SPIRITUAL CONDITION OF NIG.

"What are our joys but dreams? and what our hopes
But goodly shadows in the summer cloud?"

H. K. W.

JAMES did not improve as was hoped. Month after month passed away, and brought no prospect of returning health. He could not walk far from the house for want of strength; but he loved to sit with Aunt Abby in her quiet room, talking of unseen glories, and heart-experiences, while planning for the spiritual benefit of those around them. In these confidential interviews, Frado was never omitted. They would discuss the prevalent opinion of the public, that people of color are really inferior; incapable of cultivation and refinement. They would glance at the qualities of Nig, which promised so much if rightly directed. "I wish you would take her, James, when you are well, home with *you*," said Aunt Abby, in one of these seasons.

" Just what I am longing to do, Aunt Abby.
Susan is just of my mind, and we intend to take
her; I have been wishing to do so for years."

" She seems much affected by what she hears
at the evening meetings, and asks me many
questions on serious things; seems to love to
read the Bible; I feel hopes of her."

"I hope she *is* thoughtful; no one has a kinder
heart, one capable of loving more devotedly.
But to think how prejudiced the world are towards her people; that she must be reared in
such ignorance as to drown all the finer feelings.
When I think of what she might be, of what she
will be, I feel like grasping time till opinions
change, and thousands like her rise into a noble
freedom. I have seen Frado's grief, because she
is black, amount to agony. It makes me sick to
recall these scenes. Mother pretends to think
she don't know enough to sorrow for anything;
but if she could see her as I have, when she sup-
posed herself entirely alone, except her little dog
Fido, lamenting her loneliness and complexion, I
think, if she is not past feeling, she would retract.
In the summer I was walking near the barn, and
as I stood I heard sobs. 'Oh! oh!' I heard,

'why was I made? why can't I die? Oh, what
have I to live for? No one cares for me only to
get my work. And I feel sick; who cares for
that? Work as long as I can stand, and then
fall down and lay there till I can get up. No
mother, father, brother or sister to care for me,
and then it is, You lazy nigger, lazy nigger — all
because I am black! Oh, if I could die!'

"I stepped into the barn, where I could see
her. She was crouched down by the hay with
her faithful friend Fido, and as she ceased speak-
ing, buried her face in her hands, and cried bitterly; then, patting Fido, she kissed him, saying,
'You love me, Fido, don't you? but we must go
work in the field.' She started on her mission;
I called her to me, and told her she need not go,
the hay was doing well.

"She has such confidence in me that she will
do just as I tell her; so we found a seat under
a shady tree, and there I took the opportunity to
combat the notions she seemed to entertain
respecting the loneliness of her condition and
want of sympathizing friends. I assured her that
mother's views were by no means general; that
in our part of the country there were thousands

upon thousands who favored the elevation of her race, disapproving of oppression in all its forms; that she was not unpitied, friendless, and utterly despised; that she might hope for better things in the future. Having spoken these words of comfort, I rose with the resolution that if I recovered my health I would take her home with me, whether mother was willing or not."

"I don't know what your mother would do without her; still, I wish she was away."

Susan now came for her long absent husband, and they returned home to their room.

The month of November was one of great anxiety on James's account. He was rapidly wasting away.

A celebrated physician was called, and performed a surgical operation, as a last means. Should this fail, there was no hope. Of course he was confined wholly to his room, mostly to his bed. With all his bodily suffering, all his anxiety for his family, whom he might not live to protect, he did not forget Frado. He shielded her from many beatings, and every day imparted religious instructions. No one, but his wife, could move him so easily as Frado; so that in addition to her daily toil she was often deprived of her rest at night.

Yet she insisted on being called; she wished to show her love for one who had been such a friend to her. Her anxiety and grief increased as the probabilities of his recovery became doubtful.

Mrs. Bellmont found her weeping on his account, shut her up, and whipped her with the raw-hide, adding an injunction never to be seen snivelling again because she had a little work to do. She was very careful never to shed tears on his account, in her presence, afterwards.

CHAPTER VIII.

VISITOR AND DEPARTURE.

— " Other cares engross me, and my tired soul with emulative haste,
Looks to its God."

THE brother associated with James in business, in Baltimore, was sent for to confer with one who might never be able to see him there.

James began to speak of life as closing; of heaven, as of a place in immediate prospect; of aspirations, which waited for fruition in glory. His brother, Lewis by name, was an especial favorite of sister Mary; more like her, in disposition and preferences than James or Jack.

He arrived as soon as possible after the request, and saw with regret the sure indications of fatality in his sick brother, and listened to his admonitions — admonitions to a Christian life — with tears, and uttered some promises of attention to the subject so dear to the heart of James.

How gladly he would have extended healing

aid. But, alas! it was not in his power; so, after listening to his wishes and arrangements for his family and business, he decided to return home.

Anxious for company home, he persuaded his father and mother to permit Mary to attend him. She was not at all needed in the sick room; she did not choose to be useful in the kitchen, and then she was fully determined to go.

So all the trunks were assembled and crammed with the best selections from the wardrobe of herself and mother, where the last-mentioned articles could be appropriated.

"Nig was never so helpful before," Mary remarked, and wondered what had induced such a change in place of former sullenness.

Nig was looking further than the present, and congratulating herself upon some days of peace, for Mary never lost opportunity of informing her mother of Nig's delinquincies, were she otherwise ignorant.

Was it strange if she were officious, with such relief in prospect?

The parting from the sick brother was tearful and sad. James prayed in their presence for their renewal in holiness; and urged their immediate attention to eternal realities, and gained a promise that Susan and Charlie should share their kindest regards.

No sooner were they on their way, than Nig slyly crept round to Aunt Abby's room, and tiptoeing and twisting herself into all shapes, she exclaimed, —

"She's gone, Aunt Abby, she's gone, fairly gone;" and jumped up and down, till Aunt Abby feared she would attract the notice of her mistress by such demonstrations.

"Well, she's gone, gone, Aunt Abby. I hope she'll never come back again."

"No! no! Frado, that's wrong! you would be wishing her dead; that won't do."

"Well, I'll bet she'll never come back again; somehow, I feel as though she wouldn't."

"She is James's sister," remonstrated Aunt Abby.

"So is our cross sheep just as much, that I ducked in the river; I'd like to try my hand at curing *her* too."

"But you forget what our good minister told us last week, about doing good to those that hate us."

"Did n't I do good, Aunt Abby, when I washed and ironed and packed her old duds to get rid of her, and helped her pack her trunks, and run here and there for her?"

"Well, well, Frado; you must go finish your work, or your mistress will be after you, and remind you severely of Miss Mary, and some others beside."

Nig went as she was told, and her clear voice was heard as she went, singing in joyous notes the relief she felt at the removal of one of her tormentors.

Day by day the quiet of the sick man's room was increased. He was helpless and nervous; and often wished change of position, thereby hoping to gain momentary relief. The calls upon Frado were consequently more frequent, her nights less tranquil. Her health was impaired by lifting the sick man, and by drudgery in the kitchen. Her ill health she endeavored to conceal from James, fearing he might have less repose if there should be a change of attendants; and Mrs. Bellmont, she well knew, would have no sympathy for her. She was at last so much reduced as to be unable to stand erect for any great length of time. She would *sit* at the table to wash her dishes; if she heard the well-known step of her mistress, she would rise till she returned to her room, and then sink down for further rest. Of course she was longer than usual in completing the services assigned her. This was a subject of complaint to Mrs. Bellmont; and Frado endeavored to throw off all appearance of sickness in her presence.

But it was increasing upon her, and she could no longer hide her indisposition. Her mistress entered one day, and finding her seated, commanded her to go to work. "I am sick," replied Frado, rising and walking slowly to her unfinished task, "and cannot stand long, I feel so bad."

Angry that she should venture a reply to her command, she suddenly inflicted a blow which lay the tottering girl prostrate on the floor. Excited by so much indulgence of a dangerous passion, she seemed left to unrestrained malice; and snatching a towel, stuffed the mouth of the sufferer, and beat her cruelly.

Frado hoped she would end her misery by whipping her to death. She bore it with the hope of a martyr, that her misery would soon close. Though her mouth was muffled, and the sounds much stifled, there was a sensible commotion, which James' quick ear detected.

"Call Frado to come here," he said faintly, "I have not seen her to-day."

Susan retired with the request to the kitchen, where it was evident some brutal scene had just been enacted.

Mrs. Bellmont replied that she had "some work to do just now; when that was done, she might come."

Susan's appearance confirmed her husband's fears, and he requested his father, who sat by the bedside, to go for her. This was a messenger, as James well knew, who could not be denied; and the girl entered the room, sobbing and faint with anguish.

James called her to him, and inquired the cause of her sorrow. She was afraid to expose the cruel author of her misery, lest she should provoke new attacks. But after much entreaty, she told him all, much which had escaped his watchful ear. Poor James shut his eyes in silence, as if pained to forgetfulness by the re-

cital. Then turning to Susan, he asked her to
take Charlie, and walk out; "she needed the
fresh air," he said. "And say to mother I wish
Frado to sit by me till you return. I think you
are fading, from staying so long in this sick
room." Mr. B. also left, and Frado was thus left
alone with her friend. Aunt Abby came in to
make her daily visit, and seeing the sick countenance of the attendant, took her home with
her to administer some cordial. She soon returned, however, and James kept her with him
the rest of the day; and a comfortable night's
repose following, she was enabled to continue, as
usual, her labors. James insisted on her attend-
ing religious meetings in the vicinity with Aunt
Abby.

Frado, under the instructions of Aunt Abby
and the minister, became a believer in a future
existence — one of happiness or misery. Her
doubt was, *is* there a heaven for the black? She
knew there was one for James, and Aunt Abby,
and all good white people; but was there any
for blacks? She had listened attentively to all
the minister said, and all Aunt Abby had told
her; but then it was all for white people.

As James approached that blessed world, she felt a strong desire to follow, and be with one who was such a dear, kind friend to her.

While she was exercised with these desires and aspirations, she attended an evening meeting with Aunt Abby, and the good man urged all, young or old, to accept the offers of mercy, to receive a compassionate Jesus as their Saviour. " Come to Christ," he urged, " all, young or old, white or black, bond or free, come all to Christ for pardon ; repent, believe."

This was the message she longed to hear; it seemed to be spoken for her. But he had told them to repent; "what was that?" she asked. She knew she was unfit for any heaven, made for whites or blacks. She would gladly repent, or do anything which would admit her to share the abode of James.

Her anxiety increased; her countenance bore marks of solicitude unseen before; and though she said nothing of her inward contest, they all observed a change.

James and Aunt Abby hoped it was the springing of good seed sown by the Spirit of God. Her tearful attention at the last meeting encouraged his aunt to hope that her mind was awakened, her conscience aroused. Aunt Abby noticed that she was particularly engaged in reading the Bible; and this strengthened her conviction that a heavenly Messenger was striving with her. The neighbors dropped in to inquire after the sick, and also if Frado was "*serious?*" They noticed she seemed very thoughtful and tearful at the meetings. Mrs. Reed was very inquisitive; but Mrs. Bellmont saw no appearance of change for the better. She did not feel responsible for her spiritual culture, and hardly believed she had a soul.

Nig was in truth suffering much; her feelings were very intense on any subject, when once aroused. She read her Bible carefully, and as often as an opportunity presented, which was when entirely secluded in her own apartment, or by Aunt Abby's side, who kindly directed her to Christ, and instructed her in the way of salvation.

Mrs. Bellmont found her one day quietly reading her Bible. Amazed and half crediting the reports of officious neighbors, she felt it was time to interfere. Here she was, reading and shedding tears over the Bible. She ordered her to put up the book, and go to work, and not be snivelling about the house, or stop to read again.

But there was one little spot seldom penetrated by her mistress' watchful eye : this was her room, uninviting and comfortless; but to herself a safe retreat. Here she would listen to the pleadings of a Saviour, and try to penetrate the veil of doubt and sin which clouded her soul, and long to cast off the fetters of sin, and rise to the communion of saints.

Mrs. Bellmont, as we before said, did not trouble herself about the future destiny of her servant. If she did what she desired for *her* benefit, it was all the responsibility she acknowledged. But she seemed to have great aversion to the notice Nig would attract should she become pious. How could she meet this case? She resolved to make her complaint to John. Strange, when she was always foiled in this direction, she should resort to him. It was time something was done; she had begun to read the Bible openly.

The night of this discovery, as they were

retiring, Mrs. Bellmont introduced the conversation, by saying:

"I want your attention to what I am going to say. I have let Nig go out to evening meetings a few times, and, if you will believe it, I found her reading the Bible to-day, just as though she expected to turn pious nigger, and preach to white folks. So now you see what good comes of sending her to school. If she should get converted she would have to go to meeting: at least, as long as James lives. I wish he had not such queer notions about her. It seems to trouble him to know he must die and leave her. He says if he should get well he would take her home with him, or educate her here. Oh, how awful! What can the child mean? So careful, too, of her! He says we shall ruin her health making her work so hard, and sleep in such a place. O, John! do you think he is in his right mind?"

"Yes, yes; she is slender."

"Yes, *yes!*" she repeated sarcastically, "you know these niggers are just like black snakes; you *can't* kill them. If she wasn't tough she would have been killed long ago. There was never one of my girls could do half the work."

"Did they ever try?" interposed her husband. "I think she can do more than all of them together."

"What a man!" said she, peevishly. "But I want to know what is going to be done with her about getting pious?"

"Let her do just as she has a mind to. If it is a comfort to her, let her enjoy the privilege of being good. I see no objection."

"I should think *you* were crazy, sure. Don't you know that every night she will want to go toting off to meeting? and Sundays, too? and you know we have a great deal of company Sundays, and she can't be spared."

"I thought you Christians held to going to church," remarked Mr. B.

"Yes, but who ever thought of having a nigger go, except to drive others there? Why, according to you and James, we should very soon have her in the parlor, as smart as our own girls. It's of no use talking to you or James. If you should go on as you would like, it would not be six months before she would be leaving me; and that won't do. Just think how much profit she was to us last summer. We had no work hired out; she did the work of two girls —"

"And got the whippings for two with it!" remarked Mr. Bellmont.

"I'll beat the money out of her, if I can't get her worth any other way," retorted Mrs. B. sharply. While this scene was passing, Frado was trying to utter the prayer of the publican, "God be merciful to me a sinner."

CHAPTER IX.

DEATH.

> We have now
> But a small portion of what men call time,
> To hold communion.

SPRING opened, and James, instead of rallying, as was hoped, grew worse daily. Aunt Abby and Frado were the constant allies of Susan. Mrs. Bellmont dared not lift him. She was not "strong enough," she said.

It was very offensive to Mrs. B. to have Nab about James so much. She had thrown out many a hint to detain her from so often visiting the sick-room; but Aunt Abby was too well accustomed to her ways to mind them. After various unsuccessful efforts, she resorted to the following expedient. As she heard her cross the entry below, to ascend the stairs, she slipped out and held the latch of the door which led into the upper entry.

"James does not want to see you, or any one else," she said.

Aunt Abby hesitated, and returned slowly to her own room; wondering if it were really James' wish not to see her. She did not venture again that day, but still felt disturbed and anxious about him. She inquired of Frado, and learned that he was no worse. She asked her if James did not wish her to come and see him; what could it mean?

Quite late next morning, Susan came to see what had become of her aunt.

"Your mother said James did not wish to see me, and I was afraid I tired him."

Why, aunt, that is a mistake, I *know*. W at could mother mean?" asked Susan.

The next time she went to the sitting-room she asked her mother, —

"Why does not Aunt Abby visit James as she has done? Where is she?"

"At home. I hope that she will stay there," was the answer.

"I should think she would come in and see James," continued Susan.

"I told her he did want to see her, and to stay out. You need make no stir about it; remember:" she added, with one of her fiery glances.

Susan kept silence. It was a day or two before James spoke of her absence. The family were at dinner, and Frado was watching beside him. He inquired the cause of her absence, and *she* told him all. After the family returned he sent his wife for her. When she entered, he took her hand, and said, "Come to me often, Aunt. Come any time, — I am always glad to see you. I have but a little longer to be with you, — come often, Aunt. Now please help lift me up, and see if I can rest a little."

Frado was called in, and Susan and Mrs. B. all attempted; Mrs. B. was too weak; she did not feel able to lift so much. So the three succeeded in relieving the sufferer.

Frado returned to her work. Mrs. B. followed. Seizing Frado, she said she would " cure her of tale-bearing," and, placing the wedge of wood between her teeth, she beat her cruelly with the raw-hide. Aunt Abby heard the blows, and came to see if she could hinder them.

Surprised at her sudden appearance, Mrs. B. suddenly stopped, but forbade her removing the wood till she gave her permission, and commanded Nab to go home.

She was thus tortured when Mr. Bellmont came in, and, making inquiries which she did not, because she could not, answer, approached her; and seeing her situation, quickly removed the instrument of torture, and sought his wife. Their conversation we will omit; suffice it to say, a storm raged which required many days to exhaust its strength.

Frado was becoming seriously ill. She had no relish for food, and was constantly over-worked, and then she had such solicitude about the future. She wished to pray for pardon. She did try to pray. Her mistress had told her it would "do no good for her to attempt prayer; prayer was for whites, not for blacks. If she minded her mistress, and did what she com-manded, it was all that was required of her."

This did not satisfy her, or appease her long-ings. She knew her instructions did not har-monize with those of the man of God or Aunt Abby's. She resolved to persevere. She said nothing on the subject, unless asked. It was evident to all her mind was deeply exercised. James longed to speak with her alone on the subject. An opportunity presented soon, while the· family were at tea. It was usual to summon Aunt Abby to keep company with her, as his death was expected hourly.

As she took her accustomed seat, he asked, "Are you afraid to stay with me alone, Frado?"

"No," she replied, and stepped to the window to conceal her emotion.

"Come here, and sit by me; I wish to talk with you."

She approached him, and, taking her hand, he remarked:

"How poor you are, Frado! I want to tell you that I fear I shall never be able to talk with you again. It is the last time, perhaps, I shall *ever* talk with you. You are old enough to remember my dying words and profit by them. I have been sick a long time; I shall die pretty soon. My Heavenly Father is calling me home. Had it been his will to let me live I should take you to live with me; but, as it is, I shall go and leave you. But, Frado, if you will be a good girl, and love and serve God, it will be but a short time before we are in a *heavenly* home together. There will never be any sickness or sorrow there."

Frado, overcome with grief, sobbed, and buried her face in his pillow. She expected he would die; but to hear him speak of his departure himself was unexpected.

"Bid me good bye, Frado."

She kissed him, and sank on her knees by his bedside; his hand rested on her head; his eyes were closed; his lips moved in prayer for this disconsolate child.

His wife entered, and interpreting the scene, gave him some restoratives, and withdrew for a short time.

It was a great effort for Frado to cease sobbing; but she dared not be seen below in tears; so she choked her grief, and descended to her usual toil. Susan perceived a change in her husband. She felt that death was near.

He tenderly looked on her, and said, " Susan, my wife, our farewells are all spoken. I feel prepared to go. I shall meet you in heaven. Death is indeed creeping fast upon me. Let me see them all once more. Teach Charlie the way to heaven; lead him up as you come."

The family all assembled. He could not talk as he wished to them. He seemed to

sink into unconsciousness. They watched him
for hours. He had labored hard for breath
some time, when he seemed to awake suddenly, and exclaimed, "Hark! do you hear
it?"

"Hear what, my son?" asked the father.

"Their call. Look, look, at the shining
ones! Oh, let me go and be at rest!"

As if waiting for this petition, the Angel of
Death severed the golden thread, and he was
in heaven. At midnight the messenger came.

They called Frado to see his last struggle.
Sinking on her knees at the foot of his bed,
she buried her face in the clothes, and wept
like one inconsolable. They led her from the
room. She seemed to be too much absorbed
to know it was necessary for her to leave.
Next day she would steal into the chamber
as often as she could, to weep over his remains,
and ponder his last words to her. She moved
about the house like an automaton. Every
duty performed—but an abstraction from all,
which shewed her thoughts were busied else-
where. Susan wished her to attend his burial
as one of the family. Lewis and Mary and

Jack it was not thought best to send for, as the season would not allow them time for the journey. Susan provided her with a dress for the occasion, which was her first intimation that she would be allowed to mingle her grief with others.

The day of the burial she was attired in her mourning dress; but Susan, in her grief, had forgotten a bonnet.

She hastily ransacked the closets, and found one of Mary's, trimmed with bright pink ribbon.

It was too late to change the ribbon, and she was unwilling to leave Frado at home; she knew it would be the wish of James she should go with her. So tying it on, she said, "Never mind, Frado, you shall see where our dear James is buried." As she passed out, she heard the whispers of the by-standers, "Look there! see there! how that looks, — a black dress and a pink ribbon!"

Another time, such remarks would have wounded Frado. She had now a sorrow with which such were small in comparison.

As she saw his body lowered in the grave she wished to share it; but she was not fit to die. She could not go where he was if she did. She did not love God; she did not serve him or know how to.

She retired at night to mourn over her unfitness for heaven, and gaze out upon the stars, which, she felt, studded the entrance of heaven, above which James reposed in the bosom of Jesus, to which her desires were hastening. She wished she could see God, and ask him for eternal life. Aunt Abby had taught her that He was ever looking upon her. Oh, if she could see him, or hear him speak words of forgiveness. Her anxiety increased; her health seemed impaired, and she felt constrained to go to aunt Abby and tell her all about her conflicts.

She received her like a returning wanderer; seriously urged her to accept of Christ; explained the way; read to her from the Bible, and remarked upon such passages as applied to her state. She warned her against stifling that voice which was calling her to heaven; echoed the farewell words of James, and told her to come to her with her difficulties, and not to delay a duty so important as attention to the truths of religion, and her soul's interests.

Mrs. Bellmont would occasionally give instruction, though far different. She would tell her she could not go where James was; she need not try. If she should get to heaven at all, she would never be as high up as he.

He was the attraction. Should she "want to go there if she could not see him?"

Mrs. B. seldom mentioned her bereavement, unless in such allusion to Frado. She donned her weeds from custom; kept close her crape veil for so many Sabbaths, and abated nothing of her characteristic harshness.

The clergyman called to minister consolation to the afflicted widow and mother. Aunt Abby seeing him approach the dwelling, knew at once the object of his visit, and followed him to the parlor, unasked by Mrs. B! What a daring affront! The good man dispensed the consolations, of which he was steward, to the apparently grief-smitten mother, who talked like one schooled in a heavenly atmosphere. Such resignation expressed, as might have graced the trial of the holiest. Susan, like a mute sufferer, bared her soul to his sympathy and godly counsel, but only replied to his questions in short syllables. When he offered prayer, Frado stole to the door that she might hear of the heavenly bliss of one who was her friend on earth. The prayer caused profuse weeping, as any tender reminder of the heaven-born was sure to. When the good man's voice ceased, she returned to her toil, carefully removing all trace of sorrow. Her mistress soon followed, irritated by Nab's impudence in presenting herself unasked in the parlor, and upraided her with indolence, and bade her apply herself more diligently. Stung by unmerited rebuke, weak from sorrow and anxiety, the tears rolled down her dark face, soon followed by sobs, and then losing all control of herself, she wept aloud. This was an act of disobedience. Her mistress grasping her raw-hide, caused a longer flow of tears, and wounded a spirit that was craving healing mercies.

CHAPTER X.

PERPLEXITIES.—ANOTHER DEATH.

Neath the billows of the ocean,
Hidden treasures wait the hand,
That again to light shall raise them
With the diver's magic wand.

G. W. COOK.

THE family, gathered by James' decease, returned to their homes. Susan and Charles returned to Baltimore. Letters were received from the absent, expressing their sympathy and grief. The father bowed like a "bruised reed," under the loss of his beloved son. He felt desirous to die the death of the righteous; also, conscious that he was unprepared, he resolved to start on the narrow way, and some time solicit entrance through the gate which leads to the celestial city. He acknowledged his too ready acquiescence with Mrs. B., in permitting Frado to be deprived of her only religious privileges for weeks together. He accordingly asked his sister to take her to meeting once more, which she was ready at once to do.

The first opportunity they once more attended meeting together. The minister conversed faithfully with every person present. He was surprised to find the little colored girl so solicitous, and kindly directed her to the flowing fountain where she might wash and be clean. He inquired of the origin of her anxiety, of her progress up to this time, and endeavored to make Christ, instead of James, the attraction of Heaven. He invited her to come to his house, to speak freely her mind to him, to pray much, to read her Bible often.

The neighbors, who were at meeting,—among them Mrs. Reed,— discussed the opinions Mrs. Bellmont would express on the subject. Mrs. Reed called and informed Mrs. B. that her colored girl "related her experience the other night at the meeting."

" What experience ?" asked she, quickly, as if she expected to hear the number of times she had whipped Frado, and the number of lashes set forth in plain Arabic numbers.

"Why, you know she is serious, don't you? She told the minister about it."

Mrs. B. made no reply, but changed the subject adroitly. Next morning she told Frado she "should not go out of the house for one while, except on errands; and if she did not stop trying to be religious, she would whip her to death."

Frado pondered; her mistress was a professor of religion; was *she* going to heaven? then she did not wish to go. If she should be near James, even, she could not be happy with those fiery eyes watching her ascending path. She resolved to give over all thought of the future world, and strove daily to put her anxiety far from her.

Mr. Bellmont found himself unable to do what James or Jack could accomplish for her. He talked with her seriously, told her he had seen her many times punished undeservedly; he did not wish to have her saucy or disrespectful, but when she was *sure* she did not deserve a whipping, to avoid it if she could. "You are looking sick," he added, "you cannot endure beating as you once could."

It was not long before an opportunity offered of profiting by his advice. She was sent for wood, and not returning as soon as Mrs. B. calculated, she followed her, and, snatching from the pile a stick, raised it over her.

"Stop!" shouted Frado, "strike me, and I'll never work a mite more for you;" and throwing down what she had gathered, stood like one who feels the stirring of free and independent thoughts.

By this unexpected demonstration, her mistress, in amazement, dropped her weapon, desisting from her purpose of chastisement. Frado walked towards the house, her mistress following with the wood she herself was sent after. She did not know, before, that she had a power to ward off assaults. Her triumph in seeing her enter the door with *her* burden, repaid her for much of her former suffering.

It was characteristic of Mrs. B. never to rise in her majesty, unless she was sure she should be victorious.

This affair never met with an "after clap," like many others.

Thus passed a year. The usual amount of

scolding, but fewer whippings. Mrs. B. longed
once more for Mary's return, who had been
absent over a year; and she wrote imperatively
for her to come quickly to her. A letter came
in reply, announcing that she would comply as
soon as she was sufficiently recovered from an
illness which detained her.

No serious apprehensions were cherished by
either parent, who constantly looked for notice
of her arrival, by mail. Another letter brought
tidings that Mary was seriously ill; her mother's
presence was solicited.

She started without delay. Before she reached
her destination, a letter came to the parents
announcing her death.

No sooner was the astounding news received,
than Frado rushed into Aunt Abby's, exclaiming: —

"She's dead, Aunt Abby!"

"Who?" she asked, terrified by the unpre-
faced announcement.

"Mary; they've just had a letter."

As Mrs. B. was away, the brother and sister
could freely sympathize, and she sought him in
this fresh sorrow, to communicate such solace as

she could, and to learn particulars of Mary's untimely death, and assist him in his journey thither.

It seemed a thanksgiving to Frado. Every hour or two she would pop in into Aunt Abby's room with some strange query:

"She got into the *river* again, Aunt Abby, did n't she; the Jordan is a big one to tumble into, any how. S'posen she goes to hell, she 'll be as black as I am. Would n't mistress be mad to see her a nigger!" and others of a similar stamp, not at all acceptable to the pious, sympathetic dame; but she could not evade them.

The family returned from their sorrowful journey, leaving the dead behind. Nig looked for a change in her tyrant; what could subdue her, if the loss of her idol could not?

Never was Mrs. B. known to shed tears so profusely, as when she reiterated to one and another the sad particulars of her darling's sickness and death. There was, indeed, a season of quiet grief; it was the lull of the fiery elements. A few weeks revived the former tempests, and so at variance did they seem with chastisement sanctified, that Frado felt them to be unbearable. She determined to flee. But where? Who would take her? Mrs. B. had always represented her ugly. Perhaps every one thought her so. Then no one would take her. She was black, no one would love her. She might have to return, and then she would be more in her mistress' power than ever.

She remembered her victory at the wood-pile. She decided to remain to do as well as she could; to assert her rights when they were trampled on; to return once more to her meeting in the evening, which had been prohibited. She had learned how to conquer; she would not abuse the power while Mr. Bellmont was at home.

But had she not better run away? Where? She had never been from the place far enough to decide what course to take. She resolved to speak to Aunt Abby. *She* mapped the dangers of her course, her liability to fail in finding so good friends as John and herself. Frado's mind was busy for days and nights. She contemplated administering poison to her mistress, to rid herself and the house of so detestable a plague.

But she was restrained by an overruling Providence; and finally decided to stay contentedly through her period of service, which would expire when she was eighteen years of age.

In a few months Jane returned home with her family, to relieve her parents, upon whom years and affliction had left the marks of age. The years intervening since she had left her home, had, in some degree, softened the opposition to her unsanctioned marriage with George. The more Mrs. B. had about her, the more energetic seemed her directing capabilities, and her fault-finding propensities. Her own, she had full power over; and Jane after vain endeavors, became disgusted, weary, and perplexed, and decided that, though her mother might suffer, she could not endure her home. They followed Jack to the West. Thus vanished all hopes of sympathy or relief from this source to Frado. There seemed no one capable of enduring the oppressions of the house but her. She turned to the darkness of the future with the determination previously formed, to remain until she should be eighteen. Jane begged her to follow her so soon as she should be released; but so wearied out was she by her mistress, she felt disposed to flee from any and every one having her similitude of name or feature.

CHAPTER XI.

MARRIAGE AGAIN.

Crucified the hopes that cheered me,
All that to the earth endeared me ;
Love of wealth and fame and power,
Love, — all have been crucified.

C. E.

DARKNESS before day. Jane left, but Jack was now to come again. After Mary's death he visited home, leaving a wife behind. An orphan whose home was with a relative, gentle, loving, the true mate of kind, generous Jack. His mother was a stranger to her, of course, and had perfect right to interrogate :

"Is she good looking, Jack?" asked his mother.

"Looks well to me," was the laconic reply.

"Was her *father* rich?"

"Not worth a copper, as I know of; I never asked him," answered Jack.

"Hadn't she any property? What did you marry her for," asked his mother.

"Oh, she's *worth a million* dollars, mother, though not a cent of it is in money."

"Jack! what do you want to bring such a poor being into the family, for? You'd better stay here, at home, and let your wife go. Why could n't you try to do better, and not disgrace your parents?"

"Don't judge, till you see her," was Jack's reply, and immediately changed the subject. It was no recommendation to his mother, and she did not feel prepared to welcome her cordially now he was to come with his wife. He was indignant at his mother's advice to desert her. It rankled bitterly in his soul, the bare suggestion. He had more to bring. He now came with a child also. He decided to leave the West, but not his family.

Upon their arrival, Mrs. B. extended a cold welcome to her new daughter, eyeing her dress with closest scrutiny. Poverty was to her a disgrace, and she could not associate with any thus dishonored. This coldness was felt by Jack's worthy wife, who only strove the harder to recommend herself by her obliging, winning ways.

Mrs. B. could never let Jack be with her alone without complaining of this or that deficiency in his wife.

He cared not so long as the complaints were piercing his own ears. He would not have Jenny disquieted. He passed his time in seeking employment.

A letter came from his brother Lewis, then at the South, soliciting his services. Leaving his wife, he repaired thither.

Mrs. B. felt that great restraint was removed, that Jenny was more in her own power. She wished to make her feel her inferiority; to relieve Jack of his burden if he would not do it himself. She watched her incessantly, to catch at some act of Jenny's which might be construed into conjugal unfaithfulness.

Near by were a family of cousins, one a young man of Jack's age, who, from love to his cousin, proffered all needful courtesy to his stranger relative. Soon news reached Jack that Jenny was deserting her covenant vows, and had formed an illegal intimacy with his cousin. Meantime Jenny was told by her mother-in-law that Jack did not marry her untrammelled.

He had another love whom he would be glad,
even now, if he could, to marry. It was very
doubtful if he ever came for her.

Jenny would feel pained by her unwelcome
gossip, and, glancing at her child, she decided,
however true it might be, she had a pledge
which would enchain him yet. Ere long, the
mother's inveterate hate crept out into some
neighbor's enclosure, and, caught up hastily,
they passed the secret round till it became none,
and Lewis was sent for, the brother by whom
Jack was employed. The neighbors saw her
fade in health and spirits; they found letters
never reached their destination when sent by
either. Lewis arrived with the joyful news
that he had come to take Jenny home with
him.

What a relief to her to be freed from the
gnawing taunts of her adversary.

Jenny retired to prepare for the journey, and
Mrs. B. and Henry had a long interview. Next
morning he informed Jenny that new clothes
would be necessary, in order to make her pre-
sentable to Baltimore society, and he should
return without her, and she must stay till she
was suitably attired.

Disheartened, she rushed to her room, and, after relief from weeping, wrote to Jack to come ; to have pity on her, and take her to him. No answer came. Mrs. Smith, a neighbor, watchful and friendly, suggested that she write away from home, and employ some one to carry it to the office who would elude Mrs. B., who, they very well knew, had intercepted Jenny's letter, and influenced Lewis to leave her behind. She accepted the offer, and Frado succeeded in managing the affair so that Jack soon came to the rescue, angry, wounded, and forever after alienated from his early home and his mother. Many times would Frado steal up into Jenny's room, when she knew she was tortured by her mistress' malignity, and tell some of her own encounters with her, and tell her she might "be sure it would n't kill her, for she should have died long before at the same treatment."

Susan and her child succeeded Jenny as visitors. Frado had merged into womanhood, and, retaining what she had learned, in spite of the few privileges enjoyed formerly, was striving to enrich her mind. Her school-books were her constant companions, and every leisure moment

was applied to them. Susan was delighted to
witness her progress, and some little book from
her was a reward sufficient for any task imposed, however difficult. She had her book
always fastened open near her, where she could
glance from toil to soul refreshment. The
approaching spring would close the term of
years which Mrs. B. claimed as the period of
her servitude. Often as she passed the way-
marks of former years did she pause to ponder
on her situation, and wonder if she *could* succeed
in providing for her own wants. Her health
was delicate, yet she resolved to try.

Soon she counted the time by days which
should release her. Mrs. B. felt that she could
not well spare one who could so well adapt herself to all departments—man, boy, housekeeper,
domestic, etc. She begged Mrs. Smith to talk
with her, to show her how ungrateful it would
appear to leave a home of such comfort—how
wicked it was to be ungrateful! But Frado
replied that she had had enough of such comforts; she wanted some new ones; and as it was
so wicked to be ungrateful, she would go from
temptation; Aunt Abby said "we must n't put
ourselves in the way of temptation."

Poor little Fido! She shed more tears over him than over all beside.

The morning for departure dawned. Frado engaged to work for a family a mile distant. Mrs. Bellmont dismissed her with the assurance that she would soon wish herself back again, and a present of a silver half dollar.

Her wardrobe consisted of one decent dress, without any superfluous accompaniments. A Bible from Susan she felt was her greatest treasure.

Now was she alone in the world. The past year had been one of suffering resulting from a fall, which had left her lame.

The first summer passed pleasantly, and the wages earned were expended in garments necessary for health and cleanliness. Though feeble, she was well satisfied with her progress. Shut up in her room, after her toil was finished, she studied what poor samples of apparel she had, and, for the first time, prepared her own garments.

Mrs. Moore, who employed her, was a kind friend to her, and attempted to heal her wounded spirit by sympathy and advice, bury-

ing the past in the prospects of the future.
But her failing health was a cloud no kindly
human hand could dissipate. A little light
work was all she could accomplish. A clergyman, whose family was small, sought her, and
she was removed there. Her engagement with
Mrs. Moore finished in the fall. Frado was
anxious to keep up her reputation for efficiency,
and often pressed far beyond prudence. In the
winter she entirely gave up work, and confessed
herself thoroughly sick. Mrs. Hale, soon overcome by additional cares, was taken sick also,
and now it became necessary to adopt some
measures for Frado's comfort, as well as to
relieve Mrs. Hale. Such dark forebodings as
visited her as she lay, solitary and sad, no moans
or sighs could relieve.

The family physician pronounced her case
one of doubtful issue. Frado hoped it was final.
She could not feel relentings that her former
home was abandoned, and yet, should she be in
need of succor could she obtain it from one who
would now so grudgingly bestow it? The
family were applied to, and it was decided to
take her there. She was removed to a room

built out from the main building, used formerly
as a workshop, where cold and rain found unob-
structed access, and here she fought with bitter
reminiscences and future prospects till she became reckless of her faith and hopes and person,
and half wished to end what nature seemed so
tardily to take.

Aunt Abby made her frequent visits, and at
last had her removed to her own apartment,
where she might supply her wants, and minister
to her once more in heavenly things.

Then came the family consultation.

" What is to be done with her," asked Mrs. B.,
" after she is moved there with Nab ? "

" Send for the Dr., your brother," Mr. B. replied.

" When ? "

" To-night."

" To-night ! and for her !   Wait till morning,"
she continued.

" She has waited too long now ; I think something should be done soon."

" I doubt if she is much sick," sharply interrupted Mrs. B.

" Well, we'll see what our brother thinks."

His coming was longed for by Frado, who had known him well during her long sojourn in the family; and his praise of her nice butter and cheese, from which his table was supplied, she knew he felt as well as spoke.

"You're sick, very sick," he said, quickly, after a moment's pause. "Take good care of her, Abby, or she'll never get well. All broken down."

"Yes, it was at Mrs. Moore's," said Mrs. B., "all this was done. She did but little the latter part of the time she was here."

"It was commenced longer ago than last summer. Take good care of her; she may never get well," remarked the Dr.

"We sha'n't pay you for doctoring her; you may look to the town for that, sir," said Mrs. B., and abruptly left the room.

"Oh dear! oh dear!" exclaimed Frado, and buried her face in the pillow.

A few kind words of consolation, and she was once more alone in the darkness which enveloped her previous days. Yet she felt sure they owed her a shelter and attention, when disabled, and she resolved to feel patient, and remain till she could help herself. Mrs. B. would not attend her, nor permit her domestic to stay with her at all. Aunt Abby was her sole comforter. Aunt Abby's nursing had the desired effect, and she slowly improved. As soon as she was able to be moved, the kind Mrs. Moore took her to her home again, and completed what Aunt Abby had so well commenced. Not that she was well, or ever would be; but she had recovered so far as rendered it hopeful she might provide for her own wants. The clergyman at whose house she was taken sick, was now seeking some one to watch his sick children, and as soon as he heard of her recovery, again asked for her services.

What seemed so light and easy to others, was too much for Frado; and it became necessary to ask once more where the sick should find an asylum.

All felt that the place where her declining health began, should be the place of relief; so they applied once more for a shelter.

"No," exclaimed the indignant Mrs. B.; "she she shall never come under this roof again; never! never!" she repeated, as if each repetition were a bolt to prevent admission.

One only resource; the public must pay the expense. So she was removed to the home of two maidens, (old,) who had principle enough to be willing to earn the money a charitable public disburses.

Three years of weary sickness wasted her, without extinguishing a life apparently so feeble. Two years had these maidens watched and cared for her, and they began to weary, and finally to request the authorities to remove her.

Mrs. Hoggs was a lover of gold and silver, and she asked the favor of filling her coffers by caring for the sick. The removal caused severe sickness.

By being bolstered in the bed, after a time she could use her hands, and often would ask for sewing to beguile the tedium. She had become very expert with her needle the first year of her release from Mrs. B., and she had forgotten none of her skill. Mrs. H. praised her, and as she improved in health, was anxious to employ her. She told her she could in this way replace her clothes, and as her board would be paid for, she would thus gain something.

Many times her hands wrought when her

body was in pain ; but the hope that she might yet help herself, impelled her on.

Thus she reckoned her store of means by a few dollars, and was hoping soon to come in possession, when she was startled by the announcement that Mrs. Hoggs had reported her to the physician and town officers as an impostor. That she was, in truth, able to get up and go to work.

This brought on a severe sickness of two weeks, when Mrs. Moore again sought her, and took her to her home. She had formerly had wealth at her command, but misfortune had deprived her of it, and unlocked her heart to sympathies and favors she had never known while it lasted. Her husband, defrauded of his last means by a branch of the Bellmont family, had supported them by manual labor, gone to the West, and left his wife and four young children. But she felt humanity required her to give a shelter to one she knew to be worthy of a hospitable reception. Mrs. Moore's physician was called, and pronounced her a very sick girl, and encouraged Mrs. M. to keep her and care for her, and he would see that the authorities were informed of Frado's helplessness, and pledged assistance.

Here she remained till sufficiently restored to sew again. Then came the old resolution to take care of herself, to cast off the unpleasant charities of the public.

She learned that in some towns in Massachusetts, girls make straw bonnets — that it was easy and profitable. But how should *she*, black, feeble and poor, find any one to teach her. But God prepares the way, when human agencies see no path. Here was found a plain, poor, simple woman, who could see merit beneath a dark skin; and when the invalid mulatto told her sorrows, she opened her door and her heart, and took the stranger in. Expert with the needle, Frado soon equalled her instructress; and she sought also to teach her the value of useful books; and while one read aloud to the other of deeds historic and names renowned, Frado experienced a new impulse. She felt herself capable of elevation; she felt that this book information supplied an undefined dissatisfaction she had long felt, but could not express. Every leisure moment was carefully applied to self-improvement, and a devout and Christian exterior invited confidence from the villagers. Thus she passed months of quiet, growing in the confidence of her neighbors and new found friends.

CHAPTER XII.

THE WINDING UP OF THE MATTER.

Nothing new under the sun.
SOLOMON.

A FEW years ago, within the compass of my narrative, there appeared often in some of our New England villages, professed fugitives from slavery, who recounted their personal experience in homely phrase, and awakened the indignation of non-slaveholders against brother Pro. Such a one appeared in the new home of Frado; and as people of color were rare there, was it strange she should attract her dark brother; that he should inquire her out; succeed in seeing her; feel a strange sensation in his heart towards her; that he should toy with her shining curls, feel proud to provoke her to smile and expose the ivory concealed by thin, ruby lips; that her sparkling eyes should fascinate; that he should propose; that they should marry? A short acquaintance was indeed an objection, but she saw him often, and thought she knew him. He never spoke of his enslavement to her when alone, but she felt that, like her own oppression, it was painful to disturb oftener than was needful.

He was a fine, straight negro, whose back showed no marks of the lash, erect as if it never crouched beneath a burden. There was a silent sympathy which Frado felt attracted her, and she opened her heart to the presence of love — that arbitrary and inexorable tyrant.

She removed to Singleton, her former residence, and there was married. Here were Frado's first feelings of trust and repose on human arm. She realized, for the first time, the relief of looking to another for comfortable support. Occasionally he would leave her to " lecture."

Those tours were prolonged often to weeks. Of course he had little spare money. Frado was again feeling her self-dependence, and was at last compelled to resort alone to that. Samuel was kind to her when at home, but made no provision for his absence, which was at last unprecedented.

He left her to her fate — embarked at sea,

with the disclosure that he had never seen the South, and that his illiterate harangues were humbugs for hungry abolitionists. Once more alone! Yet not alone. A still newer companionship would soon force itself upon her. No one wanted her with such prospects. Herself was burden enough; who would have an·additional one?

The horrors of her condition nearly prostrated her, and she was again thrown upon the public for sustenance. Then followed the birth of her child. The long absent Samuel unexpectedly returned, and rescued her from charity. Recovering from her expected illness, she once more commenced toil for herself and child, in a room obtained of a poor woman, but with better fortune. One so well known would not be wholly neglected. Kind friends watched her when Samuel was from home, prevented her from suffering, and when the cold weather pinched the warmly clad, a kind friend took them in, and thus preserved them. At last Samuel's business became very engrossing, and after long desertion, news reached his family that he had become a victim of yellow fever, in New Orleans.

So much toil as was necessary to sustain Frado, was more than she could endure. As soon as her babe could be nourished without his mother, she left him in charge of a Mrs. Capon, and procured an agency, hoping to recruit her health, and gain an easier livelihood for herself and child. This afforded her better maintenance than she had yet found. She passed into the various towns of the State she lived in, then into Massachusetts. Strange were some of her adventures. Watched by kidnappers, maltreated by professed abolitionists, who did n't want slaves at the South, nor niggers in their own houses, North. Faugh! to lodge one; to eat with one; to admit one through the front door; to sit next one; awful!

Traps slyly laid by the vicious to ensnare her, she resolutely avoided. In one of her tours, Providence favored her with a friend who, pitying her cheerless lot, kindly provided her with a valuable recipe, from which she might herself manufacture a useful article for her maintenance. This proved a more agreeable, and an easier way of sustenance.

And thus, to the present time, may you see

her busily employed in preparing her merchandise; then sallying forth to encounter many frowns, but some kind friends and purchasers. Nothing turns her from her steadfast purpose of elevating herself. Reposing on God, she has thus far journeyed securely. Still an invalid, she asks your symyathy, gentle reader. Refuse not, because some part of her history is unknown, save by the Omniscient God. Enough has been unrolled to demand your sympathy and aid.

Do you ask the destiny of those connected with her *early* history? A few years only have elapsed since Mr. and Mrs. B. passed into another world. As age increased, Mrs. B. became more irritable, so that no one, even her own children, could remain with her; and she was accompanied by her husband to the home of Lewis, where, after an agony in death unspeakable, she passed away. Only a few months since, Aunt Abby entered heaven. Jack and his wife rest in heaven, disturbed by no intruders; and Susan and her child are yet with the living. Jane has silver locks in place of auburn tresses, but she has the early love of Henry still, and has never regretted her exchange of lovers. Frado has passed from their memories, as Joseph from the butler's, but she will never cease to track them till beyond mortal vision.

APPENDIX.

"TRUTH is stranger than fiction;" and whoever reads the narrative of Alfrado, will find the assertion verified.

About eight years ago I became acquainted with the author of this book, and I feel it a privilege to speak a few words in her behalf. Through the instrumentality of an itinerant colored lecturer, she was brought to W——, Mass. This is an ancient town, where the mothers and daughters seek, not "wool and flax," but *straw*,— working willingly with their hands! Here she was introduced to the family of Mrs. Walker, who kindly consented to receive her as an inmate of her household, and immediately succeeded in procuring work for her as a "straw sewer." Being very ingenious, she soon acquired the art of making hats; but on account of former hard treatment, her constitution was greatly impaired, and she was subject to seasons of sickness. On this account Mrs. W. gave her a room joining her own chamber, where she could hear her faintest call. Never shall I forget the expression of her "black, but comely" face, as she came to me one day, exclaiming, "O, aunt J——, I have at last found a *home*,— and not only a home, but a *mother*. My cup runneth over. What shall I render to the Lord for all his benefits?"

Months passed on, and she was *happy*— truly happy. Her health began to improve under the genial sunshine in which she lived, and she even looked forward with *hope* — joyful hope to the future. But, alas, "it is not in man that walketh to direct his steps." One beautiful morning in the early spring of 1842, as she was taking her usual walk, she chanced to meet her old friend, the " lecturer," who brought her to W——, and with him was a fugitive slave. Young, well-formed and very handsome, he said he had been a *house-servant*, which seemed to account in some measure for his gentlemanly manners and pleasing address. The meeting was entirely accidental; but it was a sad occurrence for poor Alfrado, as her own sequel tells. Suffice it to say, an acquaintance and attachment was formed, which, in due time, resulted in marriage. In a few days she left W——, and *all* her home comforts, and took up her abode in New Hampshire. For a while everything went on well, and she dreamed not of danger; but in an evil hour he left his young and trusting wife, and embarked for sea. She knew nothing of all this, and waited for his return. But she waited in vain. Days passed, weeks passed, and he came not; then her heart failed her. She felt herself deserted at a time, when, of all others, she most needed the care and soothing attentions of a devoted husband. For a time she tried to sustain *herself,* but this was impossible. She had friends, but they were mostly of that class who are poor in the things of earth, but " rich in faith." The charity on which she depended failed at last, and there was nothing to save her from the " County House ; " *go she must.* But her feelings on her way thither, and after her arrival, can be given better in her own language ; and I trust it will be no breach of confidence if I here insert part of a letter she wrote her mother Walker, concerning the matter.

* * * " The evening before I left for my dreaded journey to the ' house ' which was to be my abode, I packed my trunk, carefully placing in it every little memento of affection received from *you* and my friends in W——, among which was the portable inkstand, pens and paper. My beautiful little Bible was laid aside, as a place nearer my heart was reserved for that. I need not tell you I slept not a moment that night. My home, my peaceful, quiet home with you, was before me. I could see my dear little room, with its pleasant eastern window opening to the morning; but more than all, I beheld *you*, my mother, gliding softly in and kneeling by my bed to read, as no one but you *can* read, ' The Lord is my shepherd, — I shall not want ' But I cannot go on, for tears blind me. For a description of the morning, and of the scant breakfast, I must wait until another time.

" We started. The man who came for me was kind as he could be, — helped me carefully into the wagon, (for I had no strength,) and drove on. For miles I spoke not a word. Then the silence would be broken by the driver uttering some sort of word the horse seemed to understand ; for he invariably quickened his pace. And so, just before nightfall, we halted at the institution, prepared for the *homeless*. With cold civility the matron received me, and bade one of the inmates shew me my room. She did so ; and I followed up two flights of stairs. I crept as I was able ; and when she said, 'Go in there,' I obeyed, asking for my trunk, which was soon placed by me. My room was furnished some like the 'prophet's chamber,' except there was no ' candlestick ; ' so when I could creep down I begged for a light, and it was granted. Then I flung myself on the bed and cried, until I could cry no longer. I rose up and tried to pray ; the Saviour seemed near. I opened my precious little Bible, and the first verse that caught my eye was — 'I am poor and needy, yet the Lord thinketh upon me.' O, my mother, could I tell you the comfort this was to me. I sat down, calm, almost happy, took my pen and wrote on the inspiration of the moment —

> " O, holy Father, by thy power,
> Thus far in life I'm brought;
> And now in this dark, trying hour,
> O God, forsake me not.

" Dids't thou not nourish and sustain
     My infancy and youth ?
Have I not testimonials plain,
     Of thy unchanging truth ?

" Though I 've no home to call my own,
     My heart shall not repine ;
The saint may live on earth unknown,
     And yet in glory shine.

" When my Redeemer dwelt below,
     He chose a lowly lot;
He came unto his own, but lo !
     His own received him not.

" Oft was the mountain his abode,
     The cold, cold earth his bed ;
The midnight moon shone softly down
     On his unsheltered head.

" But *my* head *was sheltered,* and I tried to feel thankful."
  *   *   *   *   *   *   *

Two or three letters were received after this by her friends in
W——, and then all was silent.   No one of us knew whether
she still lived or had gone to her home on high.   But it seems
she remained in this house until after the birth of her babe ;
then her faithless husband returned, and took her to some town
in New Hampshire, where, for a time, he supported her and his
little son decently well.   But again he left her as before — suddenly and unexpectedly, and she saw him no more.   Her efforts
were again successful in a measure in securing a meagre maintenance for a time ; but her struggles with poverty and sickness
were severe.   At length, a door of hope was opened.   A kind
gentleman and lady took her little boy into their own family,
and provided everything necessary for his good ; and all this without the hope of remuneration.   But let them know, they shall

be " recompensed at the resurrection of the just." God is not unmindful of this work, — this labor of love. As for the afflicted mother, she too has been remembered. The heart of a stranger was moved with compassion, and bestowed a recipe upon her for restoring gray hair to its former color. She availed herself of this great help, and has been quite successful; but her health is again falling, and she has felt herself obliged to resort to another method of procuring her bread — that of writing an Autobiography.

I trust she will find a ready sale for her interesting work ; and let all the friends who purchase a volume, remember they are doing good to one of the most worthy, and I had almost said most unfortunate, of the human family. I will only add in conclusion, a few lines, calculated to comfort and strengthen this sorrowful, homeless one. " I will help thee, saith the Lord."

> " I will help thee," promise kind,
>   Made by our High Priest above ;
> Soothing to the troubled mind,
>   Full of tenderness and love.
>
> " I will help thee " when the storm
>   Gathers dark on every side ;
> Safely from impending harm,
>   In my sheltering bosom hide.
>
> " I will help thee," weary saint,
>   Cast thy burdens *all on me ;*
> Oh, how cans't thou tire or faint,
>   While my arm encircles thee.
>
> I have pitied every tear,
>   Heard and *counted* every sigh ;
> Ever lend a gracious ear
>   To thy supplicating cry.

What though thy wounded bosom bleed,
   Pierced by affliction's dart ;
Do I not all thy sorrows heed,
   And bear thee on my heart ?

Soon will the lowly grave become
   Thy quiet resting place ;
Thy spirit find a peaceful home
   In mansions *near my face*.

There are thy robes and glittering crown,
   Outshining yonder sun ;
Soon shalt thou lay the body down,
   And put those glories on.

Long has thy golden lyre been strung,
   Which angels cannot move ;
No song to this is ever sung,
   But bleeding, dying Love.

                        ALLIDA.

To THE FRIENDS OF OUR DARK-COMPLEXIONED BRETHREN AND
SISTERS, THIS NOTE IS INTENDED.

Having known the writer of this book for a number of years,
and knowing the many privations and mortifications she has had
to pass through, I the more willingly add my testimony to the
truth of her assertions. She is one of that class, who by some
are considered not only as little lower than the angels, but far
beneath them ; but I have long since learned that we are not
to look at the color of the hair, the eyes, or the skin, for the
man or woman ; their life is the criterion we are to judge by.
The writer of this book has seemed to be a child of misfortune.

Early in life she was deprived of her parents, and all those
endearing associations to which childhood clings. Indeed, she

may be said not to have had that happy period; for, being taken from home so young, and placed where she had nothing to love or cling to, I often wonder she had not grown up a *monster;* and those very people calling themselves Christians, (the good Lord deliver me from such,) and they likewise ruined her health by hard work, both in the field and house. She was indeed a slave, in every sense of the word; and a lonely one, too.

But she has found some friends in this degraded world, that were willing to do by others as they would have others do by them; that were willing she should live, and have an existence on the earth with them. She has never enjoyed any degree of comfortable health since she was eighteen years of age, and a great deal of the time has been confined to her room and bed. She is now trying to write a book; and I hope the public will look favorably on it, and patronize the same, for she is a worthy woman.

Her own health being poor, and having a child to care for, (for, by the way, she has been married,) and she wishes to educate him; in her sickness he has been taken from her, and sent to the county farm, because she could not pay his board every week; but as soon as she was able, she took him from that *place*, and now he has a home where he is contented and happy, and where he is considered as good as those he is with. He is an intelligent, smart boy, and no doubt will make a smart man, if he is rightly managed. He is beloved by his playmates, and by all the friends of the family; for the family do not recognize those as friends who do not include him in their family, or as one of them, and his mother as a daughter — for they treat her as such; and she certainly deserves all the affection and kindness that is bestowed upon her, and they are always happy to have her visit them whenever she will. They are not wealthy, but the latch-string is always out when suffering humanity needs a shelter; the last loaf they are willing to divide with those more needy than themselves, remembering these words, Do good as we have opportunity ; and we can always find opportunity, if we have the disposition.

And now I would say, I hope those who call themselves friends of our dark-skinned brethren, will lend a helping hand, and assist our sister, not in giving, but in buying a book; the expense is trifling, and the reward of doing good is great. Our duty is to our fellow-beings, and when we let an opportunity pass, we know not what we lose. Therefore we should do with all our might what our hands find to do ; and remember the words of Him who went about doing good, that inasmuch as ye have done a good deed to one of the least of these my brethren, ye have done it to me ; and even a cup of water is not forgotten. Therefore, let us work while the day lasts, and we shall in no wise lose our reward.

MARGARETTA THORN.

MILFORD, JULY 20th, 1859.

Feeling a deep interest in the welfare of the writer of this book, and hoping that its circulation will be extensive, I wish to say a few words in her behalf. I have been acquainted with her for several years, and have always found her worthy the esteem of all friends of humanity ; one whose soul is alive to the work to which she puts her hand. . Although her complexion is a little darker than my own, I esteem it a privilege to associate with her, and assist her whenever an opportunity presents itself. It is with this motive that I write these few lines, knowing this book must be interesting to all who have any knowledge of the writer's character, or wish to have. I hope no one will refuse to aid her in her work, as she is worthy the sympathy of all Christians, and those who have a spark of humanity in their breasts.

Thinking it unnecessary for me to write a long epistle, I will close by bidding her God speed.   C. D. S.